TACET

Essential Prose Series 169

 **Canada Council Conseil des Arts
for the Arts du Canada**

 **ONTARIO ARTS COUNCIL
CONSEIL DES ARTS DE L'ONTARIO**

an Ontario government agency
un organisme du gouvernement de l'Ontario

 Canadä

Guernica Editions Inc. acknowledges the support of the Canada Council
for the Arts and the Ontario Arts Council. The Ontario Arts Council
is an agency of the Government of Ontario.

We acknowledge the financial support of the Government of Canada.

TACET

Suzanne Chiasson

GUERNICA
EDITIONS
TORONTO • BUFFALO • LANCASTER (U.K.)
2019

Michael Mirolla, general editor
Lindsay Brown, editor
David Moratto, cover and interior design
Guernica Editions Inc.
1569 Heritage Way, Oakville, (ON), Canada L6M 2Z7
2250 Military Road, Tonawanda, N.Y. 14150-6000 U.S.A.
www.guernicaeditions.com

Distributors:
University of Toronto Press Distribution,
5201 Dufferin Street, Toronto (ON), Canada M3H 5T8
Gazelle Book Services, White Cross Mills
High Town, Lancaster LA1 4XS U.K.

First edition.
Printed in Canada.

Legal Deposit—Third Quarter
Library of Congress Catalog Card Number: 2019930487
Library and Archives Canada Cataloguing in Publication
Title: Tacet / Suzanne Chiasson.
Names: Chiasson, Suzanne, 1969- author.
Series: Essential prose series ; 169.
Description: First edition. | Series statement: Essential prose series ; 169
Identifiers: Canadiana (print) 2019005042X | Canadiana (ebook)
20190050446 | ISBN 9781771834216 (softcover) |
ISBN 9781771834223 (EPUB) | ISBN 9781771834230 (Kindle)
Classification: LCC PS8605.H5245 T33 2019 | DDC C813/.6—dc23

*I do not work within the confines of any realm.
I work in the unique moment of duration.*
—ANTONIN ARTAUD

*Get yourself out of whatever cage
you find yourself in.*
—JOHN CAGE

ONE

ON ONE SIDE of town Charlotte smiled, amused by the absurd and perfect position of her body flat on the bed, as though arranged in the night by an undertaker. Legs extended, eyelids closed, hands placed one over the other, wanting a prop, a bouquet perhaps, held just below the ribcage, which expanded now as she breathed deeply. Definitely not dead. She thought about her ribs. The bones of a corset. The hull of a boat. An accordion. A paper fan. Wings. Unfolding. Refolding. She drew her knees up, sliding her feet along the smooth cotton, then pushed them straight again, pointing her toes, arching her back and stretching her arms above her head, tossing the imaginary bouquet. She curled onto her side. The sun was insisting through the heavy curtains.

On the other side of town Theo was waking up too. He fumbled on the floor for a bottle of water. He seized empty plastic bottles one by one and chucked them across the room. They clattered down the wall. He reached a little further and found a full one that had rolled under the bed. He propped himself up on one elbow and drained it. Then he threw that one at the wall too. He fell back with a sigh. It was noon and he had a few hours before he had to go to work. Usually he managed to trade off the early shift. That way he avoided all the set-up. But today he was stuck with it. At least he'd be off early and could catch up with Curtis.

Theo and Charlotte were waking up on opposite sides of the city. The fact that they had once known each other was not on their minds. It was so far from their minds that it could almost be called *forgotten*.

TWO

CHARLOTTE OPENED THE window and reached her hand out to test the air. Even in the shade of the eaves, she felt the new warmth. The day was still. The streets were empty. She watched a squirrel scratch its way up the chestnut tree and scurry to the end of a branch. It paused, turned and darted back. Fretting. Squirrels always seemed to fret, like they were working on a problem, an eternal, mystifying question of the universe. Every so often the squirrel froze, listening for sounds of danger. But there was nothing but the occasional song of a bird.

Charlotte held still. That must be Jacqueline coming up the stairs. She shivered in spite of the warm air and looked around for her cardigan. And where were her slippers? She kneeled down to check under the bed. There was a brief knock on the door. From her crouched position on the floor, she could see clear to the other side. The door swung open and a pair of feet entered the room. Loafers, tan.

"Charlotte? Are you there?"

"I'm under the bed."

"Under the bed? Why?" Jacqueline didn't wait for a response. "Your dress has arrived."

Charlotte emerged, slippers in hand, and looked at the black garment bag that Jacqueline had laid across the quilt. It reminded her of herself that morning before she had tossed the bouquet and got out of bed, herself lying flat and long like the contents of the garment bag, waiting, not yet animated, not yet sprung—a wedding gown, the suit of an undertaker, a fashion jack-in-the-box, a costume, another costume.

The two women stood across from each other, graceful and straight. They could have passed for mother and daughter. Jacqueline, at sixty-one, held herself like a perfect ballerina. Charlotte, twenty-two years younger, was slightly taller and slightly more muscular.

"It's finally summer," Charlotte said.

"Yes. You should take your lunch outside. Come and look."

As Jacqueline unzipped the garment bag, the colour yellow spilled out. She held the hanger in her left hand, and with her right, presented the dress to Charlotte. It was a pale yellow, buttery, feathery, lemony. Charlotte reached out and let the folds of fabric roll through her fingers.

"Silk," she said.

"Yes. Chiffon."

Charlotte mouthed the word *chiffon*, pushing her lips forward to achieve Jacqueline's French pronunciation. She tried it a couple times then whispered the word in English, drawing out the second vowel long and languid, southern.

"It's like a cake," Charlotte said. "Like a lemon chiffon cake."

"I haven't seen one of those since I first came to this god-forsaken country. Bridge parties and chiffon cakes, that is what I came to."

Jacqueline hooked the dress over the mirror.

Charlotte always thought it funny the way Jacqueline

complained about this godforsaken country deprived of all things good—cheese, wine, culture, taste—and yet stayed. Half her life she'd stayed.

Jacqueline opened the closet door and surveyed the rows of shoes. She selected a pair of silver sandals and placed them at the foot of the mirror. *Perfect*, Charlotte thought.

"You don't like it?" Jacqueline asked.

"No, I do. I do."

When Jacqueline was gone, Charlotte sat down on the edge of the bed. It was undeniable. The dress was gorgeous. She should try it on. Later. She'd try it on later.

She watched the silver shoes play tricks in the mirror. When she closed one eye, the shoes winked double. She sat knowing she was just sitting, not waiting for anything, no person, no job, no deadline, no call, no obligation. Just herself. A person could sit a long time like this.

The squirrel was back in the chestnut tree. Charlotte could hear the scuttle of claws.

THREE

THE ONLY LIGHT in Theo's room came from the screen of his phone. A makeshift curtain kept out the daylight: three old towels tacked up and held together with bull clips. This was temporary, Theo assured himself, until he could find the right thing. At one time the window had been covered with a shimmering sari, but the girlfriend who had put it there took it with her when she left. That, along with the kettle. She used to make tea, Theo reminisced. Every morning, tea. He could really go for a cup of tea right now.

He flipped through his messages. There were five texts and two emails just from Curtis, begging him to call. Theo typed a reply: *Bring me a coffee.*

He waited a few seconds then chuckled as he read the response: @#$%&! Curtis swore like a comic book and only relayed important information in person. Whatever he had to say wouldn't be said by text.

The phone vibrated in Theo's hand, giving him a start.

"Curtis man, what's the emergency? Where are you? What? You're in the living room? All morning? You've been up all morning? Why don't you just knock on the fucking door?"

The phone went dead, then ... a knock. Four slow, deliberate raps.

Curtis walked into the room without a word. He moved

with precision, transferring a pile of clothes from the chair to the dresser, sitting down on the chair, and crossing one leg over the other as was his habit.

Theo noticed an envelope in Curtis' hand.

"That doesn't look like my coffee," Theo said.

Curtis just smiled.

"You know I can't do anything until I have my coffee. I need to wake up."

Curtis stood and went to the window, and with one swift magician's hand, tore the towels down. Sunlight rushed. Tacks sprayed. Theo yelled and covered his eyes. And the dust from the towels tumbled and churned against the backdrop of the day.

"Are you awake now?" Curtis asked calmly.

Sadistic, Theo thought. It reminded him of something. What was that movie, that voice? The nurse.

"Ratched!" he said. "You're my Nurse Ratched. Aren't you supposed to be at work?"

"Flex day."

He had taken up his position on the chair again, still holding the envelope, tapping it on his thigh, rhythmically. Then he raised the envelope and tapped it against the air.

"This," he said, "this is what I'm talking about. This is what we've been looking for."

"You say that every time. You said that last night, and it was shit. You know who I talked to most of the night? A Kool-Aid jug." He grinned, knowing that Curtis was growing more and more impatient with him. "That's right. The jug and I, we had a heart to heart. We shared. We laughed. The jug was pleased. I could tell by the expression on its face. But the rest of them ..." He shook his head.

"This is different." Curtis held up the envelope again, "This is one hundred percent champagne."

The envelope landed on the bed. Theo saw Curtis' name written in slanted black loops. It looked awfully like a wedding invitation. He picked it up, drew out a white card. Apparently, a Madame Jacqueline Day had the pleasure of inviting Curtis to a summer *soirée*.

"You've got to be kidding me," Theo said. "Who sends stuff like this? It's ridiculous." He looked more closely. "And it's this weekend."

"Just in the nick of time. Do you know how hard it is to get one of these invitations?"

"No. I don't."

"You're coming."

"I'm working."

"You're coming."

"I'm not even invited."

But Curtis wouldn't let it go. While Theo lay on his back and shielded his eyes with the invitation, Curtis talked. He talked about opera, opportunity, jazz, glamour, filmmakers, designers, this lady who gathered it all together, surrounding herself with talent and beauty. It was the place to be, Curtis explained, the place where Theo really ought to be.

"Look at the invitation," Curtis said. "Feel the weight of it. It's gorgeous."

Theo removed the card from the bridge of his nose and looked at it. "Posers," he said. "Nothing but posers. How did you get it?"

"Grigore."

"The old Romanian?"

"Yes. And no, I'm not sleeping with him." Curtis uncrossed his legs and leaned in. "Look, I know it's not your scene. But there's something there, something more. Something …"

Theo looked out at the beautiful day, perfect for tennis. If he got up now, he could get some tennis in before going to work. He'd call Kenji. He thought about the Romanian, the something more, the thing that Curtis was trying to describe. It wasn't the money. Or the glamour. That's not what he was talking about. No, it was the way people lived, the idea that somehow these people lived with more intensity. *It's bullshit*, Theo thought. *An illusion.* He ran his thumbs over the smooth card. God, he wanted a coffee. Maybe he could convince Curtis to get him a coffee. And he was out of cigarettes. The sunshine was stunning.

"This party," Theo said. "Which one of us is the talent and which one of us is the beauty?"

"You're both, darling. You're both."

Theo tossed the invitation to the foot of the bed.

"I'm not going."

FOUR

THEO DIDN'T KNOW that by the end of the day his name would appear next to Curtis' on a guest list on the desk of Jacqueline Day. It was not unusual for the two twenty-two-year-olds to be regarded as a couple. People were so used to seeing them together that they just assumed.

Charlotte wasn't paying much attention to the list-making. She'd collected some white daisies from the garden and was rearranging the stems in her hand.

"*Ma chérie*," Jacqueline said. "You'll be happy to hear that your favourite photographer will not be attending."

"Jacob?"

"Yes, Jacob."

Charlotte was relieved. Jacob was a letch.

"Apparently," Jacqueline said, "he has a prior commitment that he'd forgotten about. A wife."

"Why doesn't he bring her?"

"I think he likes to keep things separate." Jacqueline put down her pen and turned to her laptop, glancing sideways at Charlotte for a moment. "Those flowers won't last long out of water."

"I know." Charlotte looked at the bouquet. "Did you ever make daisy chains when you were a child?"

"Daisy chains?"

"Where you string them together to make a chain, not with big ones like these, but with the tiny ones you find in the grass. See, you make a split in the middle of the stem, like this, and then you feed another stem all the way through to the head. See." She held up the two linked flowers. "And then you keep going until you have a chain long enough for a crown or a necklace."

"Now I know why I never had a child of my own. I have you. *Alors*, what are you singing on Saturday?"

"We're working something new with the Purcell. We thought we'd start with that."

"No. I've already talked to Olivier."

"Oh." Charlotte said. She tugged at the two linked daisies. They were stronger than the little ones. They held fast.

"Here, pass me those flowers." Jacqueline came around the desk and took the daisies from Charlotte. "I'll have Joy put them in water."

Charlotte rubbed her hands together and smelled her nails where they had split the stem—a green smell, fresh, bitter. She wondered how old she'd been when she'd learned to make daisy chains. Six? Seven? Was it her mother who'd taught her? A friend? A friend's mother maybe? She squinted at the memory, but it was tangled up with another of when she was a teenager, in love. The pictures were unclear, overlapping. Grass. Warm sun. Blue sky. The shade of a tree. So perfect it was hard to imagine any of it was real.

That's a shame, she thought. The Purcell was just starting to get interesting.

***

Olivier put down his coffee and greeted Charlotte with a kiss on each cheek. "So," he said matter-of-factly, "no more *One Charming Night*."

"No more," Charlotte said, noticing that her daisies were already in a vase. Joy, the housecleaner, must have done it.

"Our charming night has been vetoed," Olivier said. "It's just as well. It's heating up out there, and she wants jazz."

"Was she more specific?"

"No. She said to surprise her."

Charlotte and Olivier stood side by side, looking out through the open terrace doors. Charlotte's eyes wandered to the tops of the trees in the forest behind the garden, where the trees met the sky, dark green on light blue, like paper cut-outs pasted on, like the daisy-chain memories, too good to be true. She could tell that Olivier was not happy about the music, the way he fidgeted with his watch, shifting it back and forth, centring the watch face on his wrist repeatedly.

Over the years she'd come to know his habits, his little ways. He'd begun spending more and more time visiting Jacqueline and much less time in France until finally he was living in Vancouver ten out of twelve months. He had an apartment downtown but was at the house most of the time. Charlotte had learned to read his silent cues. When he was displeased, he fiddled, often with his watch. When he was turned on, the tips of his ears went red. When he was sad, he stared at his shoes. He wasn't staring at his shoes right now, but as usual, they were polished, and his black hair was combed.

"I have an idea," Charlotte said.

"Good," Olivier turned away from the open doors and went over to the piano. "We need an idea."

FIVE

THEO WASN'T AS good a tennis player as Kenji, but he could keep up. Today's game was going well. Yesterday had been a scramble after all that stuff with the invitation and Curtis ripping down the towels. Today Theo's head was clear. The air was clear. It was another quiet weekday in the park. And each clean crack on the racket resonated.

They took a break, and Kenji went to refill his bottle at the drinking fountain. Theo sat on the asphalt, his back against the cage, gulped down some water, and didn't smoke. He was stunned by the fresh air. Too much time in bars and basements—he had forgotten how much he liked being outside. *Why didn't he do this more often?* he wondered. Why did he waste so many mornings? Why couldn't he just do the things that were good for him? Maybe he'd start running again, maybe start lifting weights. He hated the gym, though. Maybe he could convince Curtis to chip in for some weights for the house. He should really go back to his acting workshop too, although he hated that scene almost as much as the gym. Maybe he'd look for a new group.

Kenji was back. He squeezed water into his mouth from the bottle, letting some of it trickle down his chin, then he squeezed some on his head and shook it out like a dog.

"We certainly don't need a ball boy today," he said.

"Nope." Theo took another swig. *It was the perfect drink*, he thought. That was another thing—he should cut down on the booze. "When I was a kid, I used to be my dad's ball boy, when he played with his friends."

"Did he pay you?"

"Pay me? No man, I was just a kid. I was having fun. And I liked to see how fast I could get the balls." Theo smiled at the memory then jumped to his feet. "Come on. I'm warmed up now. Let's play."

* * *

Theo went home feeling motivated. After his shower, he was going to get a coffee and make a plan.

His phone rang. It must be Curtis again, hounding him about that swank party. But when he looked at the number, he didn't recognize it.

"Hello?" It was his father. "Dad? Hi. Wow, long time." Theo struggled to get the words out.

His dad started talking. He was in town for the weekend with Sylvie. That was Theo's step-mom, although he'd never really thought of her as a mom. By the time she and his dad had gotten married, Theo had moved out. She was nice enough.

His father was explaining that they'd just arrived at the airport and were in a taxi. They were going to a wedding on a boat that evening, so they didn't have time to see him ... had to get to the hotel to freshen up. Then the next day there was a brunch and ... As Theo listened to his father, the morning drained away. He was starting to shiver from the sweat on his skin. He wanted to take a hot shower.

"So tomorrow night," his dad said, "we'd like to take you out for dinner."

"I can't." Theo didn't even hesitate.

"Are you working?"

"Yeah, but ... well ... I just have plans."

"You can change them, can't you?"

"No. I can't. Sorry, you should have given me more notice. I'm locked into this thing."

For a moment Theo wished he hadn't said it, but he had, and he didn't know how to change it. Before he even had a chance to figure it out, his father started again with a list of reasons why he should reconsider. It had been over a year since they'd seen him, they didn't know when they'd have a chance to visit again, Sylvie was really looking forward to it, his job couldn't be that important, and finally: "You don't have plans with that roommate of yours, do you?"

"Yes," Theo said. "Yes, in fact, I do." The words came out slow and steady, cold.

"What plans?"

"Nothing really. Just a little party."

There was a long pause, and finally his dad said: "Well, Sylvie will be very disappointed."

And that was the end of it. His dad and Sylvie would spend the weekend in Vancouver then fly back to Toronto without seeing him.

Theo hung up and kicked the table. It was solid oak. He growled. He banged the cap off a beer and swallowed half of it in one go, cranked the music, stood under the shower and let the hot water beat down on his head as the bathroom filled with steam. He pressed the cold bottle against his neck, relishing the contrast in temperature. He started to feel calm again, clean. The ball boy memory slipped into his thoughts. He put it out.

By the time Curtis got home, Theo was out of the shower, getting dressed, feeling composed and energized.

"Hey, that's my jacket!" Curtis said.

"How does it look? Will it do for Saturday night?" Theo turned from the mirror.

"You're coming? You're coming. Yes! I knew you would."

"With this shirt underneath. What do you think?"

"Why do you have to have such broad shoulders? It makes the jacket way too small."

"I like it that way. It's awkward. I want to look slightly awkward."

Curtis cocked his head to one side. "It works."

"What time's this thing at anyway?" Theo asked, turning back to the mirror.

"Eight-thirty. I am so glad you're coming. This is very, very good news."

"You already signed me up, didn't you?"

"I did. I had complete faith in you."

Theo was wondering if he should tell Curtis about the phone call from his dad. Maybe Curtis would help him see things from his dad's perspective as he sometimes did. But the issue was mixed up with his father's dislike for Curtis and the fact that Theo was only going to the party out of spite. Besides, he was calm now. Why get all riled up again?

Theo caught Curtis' eye in the mirror.

"What?" they said at the same time.

"Beer?" Theo asked.

That day, Theo had a knack for ending conversations.

SIX

CHARLOTTE WAS HAVING a staring contest with a coyote. She smiled at the wild dog, poised, one paw mid-stride. "There's nothing for you here," she said. "Come back this evening when the silly guests have arrived." The coyote turned away and continued trotting a path across the back lawn and into the forest.

Charlotte wondered what silly guest Jacqueline might have in mind for her that evening. There was usually someone, someone who would hang around her for a while, the two of them would make polite talk, he'd drink quite a bit, and eventually she'd give him an out, an escape route, he'd disappear into the crowd, and they'd both be relieved because it wasn't their idea in the first place.

She looked up at the house. The terrace doors were open to the day. Inside she could see Joy and one of the caterers, hands on the black marble top of the pedestal table, inching it to the middle of the room. The rugs and winter drapes had been stripped away, the hardwood polished, sheer white curtains hung. It was non-stop, and Charlotte had been kicked out after colliding with a tulip delivery while trying to make tea in the kitchen.

"Go relax in the garden," Jacqueline had said. "You must rest yourself for tonight."

Any more rest, Charlotte thought, *and I'll be dead.*

A lawn mower started up next door. She had a look over the fence. It was the gardener, the only person she ever saw there. The owners lived abroad. On the other side was an older couple. They were quiet and did their own gardening, even the lawn. They used to have a teenager from down the street come to do the lawn. He used to do Jacqueline's too. But then he went off to university. The couple's grandchildren came to stay with them for a few weeks every summer, running through sprinklers shrieking all afternoon then stopping to eat ice-cream. Charlotte hadn't heard them yet this year. Maybe it was too early. Maybe school wasn't out yet. Or maybe they'd grown too old for running through sprinklers. There weren't many kids in the neighbourhood anymore, and the ones who were there were shuttled in and out like celebrities in Mercedes with tinted windows.

Charlotte was hungry. She didn't want to go back into the house with all the activity. She knew that, if she asked, Jacqueline would bring something out to the terrace. But she didn't want to ask. She didn't want to have her lunch fixed for her.

She wandered around the side of the house. It was cooler there, shaded by the cedars and the chestnut tree, its broad, flat leaves. With the toe of her clog, she scuffed the dirt, the moss, bits of branches. She looked up. No squirrels. She took a few steps closer to the house and looked up again, feeling a bit dizzy. *It must be the lack of food*, she thought. She was standing directly below her bedroom window, which seemed so small in relation to the rest of the house. Staring straight up like that made her even dizzier, and she lost her balance and half collapsed, half sat down on the ground, where she stayed, looking around her.

There was an open patch, part dirt, part grass, that seemed to want for something. A sandbox maybe. And if there was a sandbox, there would have to be children. How odd to imagine Jacqueline's world inhabited by children. Charlotte closed her eyes. She could hear the sound of them playing in the yard—the laughing, fighting, wanting, needing, crying. Kids were loud. And messy. In Jacqueline's world, there would have to be a nanny. Charlotte looked up and considered her bedroom window again. Had her room been a nanny's room once upon a time? Before Jacqueline had moved here. It was probably too large for a nanny's room. Perhaps it had been a child's room. She stared at the window but there was no face staring back. No ghost to give her a clue. Just an empty hole, a black spot.

Charlotte hugged her knees and noticed a beetle crawling in front of her feet. She nudged it gently with a stick, then jumped up, afraid that she might be sitting on a sea of beetles. She frantically brushed off her clothes and shook out her hair, but the ground where she had been sitting was not seething with bugs. It lay still and intact.

She took one last look at the window and went inside.

SEVEN

THERE WAS A lot to see from the taxi. Theo and Curtis watched people stride out, bare legs, laughing, the rain left long behind, the patios of bars and coffee houses overflowing, people moving, released. Theo was thinking how good everyone looked. Some days he would walk around wondering why everyone looked so damned ugly, and other days it seemed like the city was full of the most gorgeous people on the planet. It all had to do with the light. That was his theory. Overcast days without rain were unforgiving. Nobody could hide. But tonight was clear, the late sun soft, and skin glowed like the new west.

Theo wasn't very comfortable though in the back of the cab. The seatbelt was rubbing against his neck and he was restless. He wanted to be on the other side, with the people on the go, instead of on his way to a stuffy *soirée*. He thought of his father out to dinner somewhere in the city and shook it off. If he could accomplish one thing that night, it would be to forget about his father.

As the taxi moved further west, the houses and yards got bigger. There were more trees and fewer people, some dog-walkers, bikes pulling trailers with empty bottles or babies inside, teenagers waiting at bus stops or trekking down to the beach in packs, hoping to make something of the night, testing it with their bravado. Through the open window, Theo listened to their yelps, their revved-up hilarity, then after a while there were no more voices on the air and nobody on the street.

The taxi turned right and slowed as it approached the address marked on the invitation, which Curtis had been holding in his lap the whole ride. There was a line of cars letting people out, and guests filed up the long, curved driveway. Curtis was muttering something as they got out of the cab, but Theo wasn't listening. He was absorbed in his new surroundings. He had expected something different, something bigger. He had expected Roman pillars and a fountain in the middle of the lawn, with coloured lights, and a great big gate at the front, with a guard. Maybe it was all Curtis' talk about the opera the other day, but he had expected something grander.

He watched the guests funnel in through the open door at the top of the steps, into the light of the house. It looked like a cottage. White paint. Green shutters. Tall hedges at the front. The forest behind. And to the left of the driveway, a lawn that rolled down to his feet.

"Do you think I'll need this?" Curtis whacked Theo's arm with the invitation.

"No, put it away." They started walking up the drive.

"Do you think I'm overdressed?" Curtis asked, inspecting his tuxedo.

"No, you look perfect."

"How do you know? You didn't even look."

"What are you, my goddamn date? Honey, you're beautiful. In fact you've never looked so good. How's that?"

"I'll take it. And speaking of dates, that's mine just inside the door."

"The old Romanian? I thought you said ..." Theo followed Curtis up the steps and inside, squeezing his way through. The entranceway buzzed like opening night.

Grigore swung an arm around Curtis, shook him affectionately, and introduced him to their hostess, who was greeting everyone as they came in. Then it was Theo's turn, and he took Jacqueline's outstretched hand, and it was a different kind of handshake. She put her other hand gently over his so that she was holding it between both of hers, briefly, warmly.

"Enjoy," she said, then let go and turned to welcome someone else.

Theo felt a bit stupid. He hadn't said a word, not even *hello*. He stood off to the side and watched her for a minute clasping hands, kissing cheeks. She never quite stopped, never broke her motion. She caught him watching, smiled slightly as she kept talking to the person in front of her, and Theo figured it was time to move on.

He followed a hallway into a vast, glamorous room. Definitely not a cottage. A server held a tray out to Theo and he took a glass. He surveyed the crowd, looking for Curtis, who had taken off with Grigore. *There sure are a lot of old people*, he thought. He rooted himself next to a big round table, sipped the champagne and hoped that no one would talk to him. He couldn't see Curtis anywhere. The room wandered, stretched, doorways and halls, a baby grand at the foot of the staircase, clusters of guests with glasses in hand, and everything polished. Theo checked his phone—nothing interesting—and stared at the mass of flowers in the middle of the big round table. He'd never seen so many flowers in one spot. The colour was crazy, saturated, and he thought it would be a good moment to smoke some weed, but that would have to wait. He drank the champagne, smiling to himself. This was the beginning of the forgetting.

Theo found Curtis on the terrace with Grigore and some of his entourage. He lit a cigarette and hovered, half-listening, then drew Curtis away.

"What is it?" Curtis whispered.

"You took off."

"You said I wasn't your date."

"What are you doing with this guy?"

"Seriously? Half an hour and you'll be making out with some girl in the gazebo."

Theo looked around the backyard. "There is no gazebo."

"It's a figure of speech."

"No, it's not."

Curtis returned to the Grigore conversation. Theo helped himself to another glass of champagne from a passing tray and sat down in a wicker chair with cushions covered in palm leaves. He put his feet up and scanned the terrace like a diminutive emperor of the South Seas. *Mesh*, he thought, looking at his shoes. I should be wearing mesh shoes, *Miami Vice*, old school. He laughed out loud, flicked his cigarette into a cut-glass ashtray and caught sight of a woman in a white mini skirt. "Meet me in the gazebo," he said under his breath, but she disappeared inside, didn't even look his way.

Eventually Curtis came over and sat next to him in another wicker chair, crossing his legs. They were chain-smoking, the two of them, basking in the excess, the flow. The sun was down now, and everything flickered magic.

"I was right, wasn't I?" Curtis said. "Admit it, I was right."

"You know what it is?" Theo said. "That makes it different? I'm just starting to see it." He pulled on his cigarette and let the smoke roll out. "It's easy."

"What's easy?"

"This." Theo gestured to the air with both arms outstretched. "It's so fucking easy."

* * *

Charlotte grimaced at the mirror. It grimaced back—a Brechtian mask. It made her look older, sixty-nine instead of thirty-nine. But not just older—altered—the skin pulled up to her ears, taut, grotesque. She let the mask drop and considered herself seriously. Perhaps in this little universe that Jacqueline had created, she was in fact a star. And perhaps it made sense for her to be waiting upstairs for her call, like in a dressing room. Jacqueline had put her there, all those years ago. She'd made it easy for her at a time when everything had been so difficult. She'd given Charlotte her own little spot, a home.

Petrified, Charlotte thought, considering her image. *That's what it is.* Preserved in time. In a time that didn't even belong to Charlotte. With her eyebrow pencil, she drew a beauty mark near her upper lip. It reminded her of old friends in cramped dressing rooms—elbows, razors, wigs, cigarettes, pills, perfume, panty hose, implants, and beauty marks *à la* Marilyn. Francis used to do Josephine Baker in all his leanness, and that was what Charlotte was going to sing tonight. *My Fate Is in Your Hands.*

There was a knock on the door. It was showtime.

Charlotte stepped back from her reflection. The chiffon floated. It was exquisite. The dress was so light that she felt almost naked. She checked her hair, her make-up. She was ready.

She listened to the voices downstairs, recognizing some of the laughs. She wondered if anyone could see her silver sandals on the landing and what they might look like descending from nowhere, the feet of an angel, or an alien from Mars. She lifted the hem of her dress and started down the stairs. The noise subsided, conversations broke into whispers and people came closer, gathered. Many of them knew Charlotte and knew what to expect. She took her place beside the piano, where Olivier was waiting.

At the back of the room, Curtis nudged Theo. They had just come in from the terrace.

"It's the singer," Curtis said.

"What singer?" Theo couldn't see through the crowd.

"The one who always sings."

The moment Charlotte began, Theo gasped, nearly choking on his champagne. The voice was unmistakeable. He knew it instantly. His stomach flipped. He glanced desperately at Curtis, but Curtis was staring straight ahead. Theo covered his mouth, stifling his cough. He needed to get hold of himself. He needed to calm down. He closed his eyes, and listened, and breathed. Then he opened his eyes and carefully he edged his way along the right side of the crowd, making his way to the front. He had to see her.

Charlotte was facing the guests, knowing they were there, sensing them, but seeing them only in outline, in silhouette. She sang standing still and knowing she was standing still but feeling like she was moving, turning, and there were paintings hung, strung together with nothing but the melody. And the whole thing turned like a suspended carousel, she with it. And then one of the paintings, a portrait that was not a portrait but a face, came into focus. And she saw Theo.

Theo was aware of the *cliché*. He'd seen too many movies where time stood still. But that is exactly what it felt like. For just a second, he and Charlotte were locked together, and whatever was going on around them didn't exist.

Then it was gone. The applause erupted. The piano started again. And Charlotte was taken back by the crowd.

* * *

"How do you know her?" Curtis handed Theo a cigarette.

"She was ... she was my dad's girlfriend. For a few years when I was a kid. We ... she ... well, we all lived together. Before my dad and I moved to Toronto."

"Like a family," Curtis said. "She was basically like a step-mom?"

"Yeah, basically."

Theo proceeded to get drunk. He found good company on the terrace. He chatted with a radio host who smoked a pipe and shared the same sense of humour, and the two of them spent a good hour slapping their knees and drying their tears. The music poured out. The heat of the night wouldn't back off. And behind all the jokes, Theo heard every note that Charlotte sang.

* * *

Charlotte turned her back to the room of people, fanned herself with a book and drank a glass of water. They were taking a break. Why was it so hot? The chiffon clung to her skin. She looked at Olivier in his full suit. How could he stand it? She wondered where Theo was. She hoped she hadn't scared him away.

"What is it?" Olivier asked. "Something has happened, I can tell."

She nodded. Olivier put his hand on her arm, and she told him about Theo, how he was there at the party, how she'd seen him. And she told him about Theo's father, Johann, and how he'd left her. Just packed up and moved away.

"It's a basic heartbreak story," she said. "And it was so long ago."

Olivier raised his eyebrows, indicating over her shoulder. She turned to see Jacqueline approaching with Theo on one arm and Curtis on the other. Both boys looked terrified.

Jacqueline made the introductions, and they all shook hands. Jacqueline glanced around the little circle. Nobody was saying anything. Finally, Olivier cleared his throat.

"You see," he said. "As it turns out, Charlotte and Theo are already acquainted." They were all looking at Jacqueline now, and Jacqueline was looking at Charlotte.

"Yes, it's true," Charlotte said. "I knew Theo when he was young. In fact, I used to take care of him."

Jacqueline smiled in her slight way. "You mean you were his babysitter? How quaint. And how fortunate to be reunited. How has he turned out, the little Theo? All grown up, big and strong?"

Charlotte felt embarrassed for Theo. She felt dumb.

Knotted. She wanted to say something, something smart, or just something to break the tension. Then Theo did it for her.

"I've looked like this since I was eight," he said.

Jacqueline regarded him coolly then looked at Charlotte again. "Was he always this funny?" she asked.

And everybody laughed.

Charlotte remembered Theo at eight. He *was* always funny. She had a vision of him dressed up in one of her big hats and a pair of high heels, standing on the kitchen table, singing *What if God was one of us?* at the top of his lungs.

And so it was decided that Theo would come to visit some time. And Charlotte went back to the piano with Olivier. The evening slowed, swayed. Curtis was down to his shirtsleeves. Theo was still wearing his jacket, slightly awkward. Grigore had left, and Curtis wasn't sure why.

"We should go soon, don't you think?" Curtis said to Theo.

"Why? If we go, we could wake up tomorrow and it might all be a dream. Isn't this what you've been searching for?"

"I'm not sure."

Charlotte was singing another love song and thinking how it didn't matter that Johann was long gone because Theo was here now.

EIGHT

THEO WASN'T USED to drinking scotch, especially in the afternoon. Jacqueline had handed it to him without asking, on the rocks. It seemed to be her thing, handing out drinks.

The taste was sharp, but he was glad of it. It fit. He should lean back and put his feet up on the desk, but the desk was too beautiful, he didn't want to scuff it. And his chair was too stiff and too small. And besides, this visit—waiting in Jacqueline's office while the clock ticked—was starting to feel like a job interview, where putting his feet up on the desk would not be the thing to do. Nor would lighting a cigarette, even though there was an empty amber dish on the desk that looked much more like an ashtray than a paper clip holder.

He turned his attention to the bookshelves to his right. He didn't recognize most of the titles. Many of them were in French, written the wrong way on the spine, from bottom to top. He had to lean his head to the left to read them. He wasn't much of a reader anyway. And his French was terrible.

There was an old radio on one of the shelves, which he guessed to be from the 1930s or '40s. He'd never seen anything like it in person. Only in movies. He stared at it. *Tell me a story*, he said in his head to the radio. He wanted a story from the war. He wanted crackling news announce-ments, troops marching into Paris, gunshots, the signal coming in and out so that he'd have to tweak the knobs. But the radio was silent.

The only sound came from the clock that hung on the wall behind the desk. It was already 5:20. He'd arrived just after 5. Jacqueline had led him to this room and gone to get Charlotte. What was taking them so long?

Theo couldn't get comfortable in his chair. He worried it might snap in two. He tried to guess what era it came from like he'd done for the radio, but he knew he was mixing up his periods and scenes from films, the French revolution with the 1920s. His knowledge of history was terrible. *It's old!* he thought and laughed out loud. The sound of his big laugh in the small room struck him as extra funny, and he laughed again. *The chair's really fucking old!*

He was a bit giddy, a bit nervous. He took a sip of his drink. The ice cubes clicked. The clock ticked. He looked at the desk again, wondering what kind of wood it was made of, the palest, smoothest wood he'd ever seen. He transferred his glass to his left hand and ran his right hand across the top of the desk. His hand was cold from the ice, and the wood was warm in contrast.

"It's Italian." Jacqueline's voice surprised him, and he pulled back his hand. "The desk," she said. "Italian de-sign. Isn't it beautiful?"

"Yes."

"You don't talk much, do you, Theo?"

He shrugged. What was he supposed to say to that?

"You remind me of cowboys. Men of few words. The

Wild West. When I first came to Canada, I loved the idea of the Wild West. Do you like Westerns?"

"Sure."

"I could never sit through a Western."

"This isn't really cowboy territory though," Theo said. "You've got to go to Alberta for that. Or at least out to the Valley."

"It's too cold in Alberta. I don't like the cold. And besides, I don't really care for cowboys anymore either. What's the expression? You can take the girl out of Paris but you can't take Paris out of the girl."

Theo tried to get a read on this girl from Paris who was far from a girl but true to the idea nonetheless and wondered why she had come to Canada in the first place. He wasn't going to ask though. He looked down at his glass. Where the hell was Charlotte?

"I checked on her," Jacqueline said. "She's still asleep."

And he wasn't going to ask how she knew he'd been thinking about Charlotte, nor why Charlotte was sleeping in the middle of the day. He was going to wait for more information, wait for Jacqueline.

"Charlotte is not like most people," she said finally.

"What do you mean?"

"She's very special. We can't expect her to do things in the normal way. Do you understand?"

"She's got her own way of doing things," Theo said.

"Yes. She does. I worry about her. Often. She's my responsibility, you see."

Theo wasn't exactly sure what Jacqueline was getting at. Was she saying that Charlotte was mentally ill?

"Is she sick?" he asked.

"No! No, no, no. She's not sick. She's just not like the rest of us. She doesn't need to concern herself with the world. That's why I'm here. You'll see. You'll talk to her and you'll see. You must come back tomorrow. She'll be so sorry she missed you."

Theo wondered why Jacqueline didn't just go and wake Charlotte up.

"Theo, what kind of work have you done?"

"Not much. A small part on a series."

"Speaking?"

"Yes."

"Commercials?"

"No."

"Stage?"

"No. Except in some of my classes. But it's been mostly film."

"And how old are you?"

"Twenty-two."

"Do you have an agent?"

"No."

Jacqueline stopped here. She looked down and smoothed the fabric of her skirt. Theo noticed that her chair wasn't old and stiff like his. It was a modern chair, black leather. And it swivelled. And she was swivelling in it now, slightly.

Jacqueline raised her head and looked him in the eye again. She leaned forward onto her elbows.

"Are you any good?" she asked.

Theo hesitated, just for effect.

"Yes," he said. "I'm good."

"Excellent. Then that's it." Jacqueline slapped the desk with both hands. "Bring me your résumé, headshots, whatever you have, and I'll take care of it."

"Seriously? You can do that?"

"Yes, I can. Bring them tomorrow so Charlotte can see you."

Jacqueline stood up. Theo followed suit, sensing that the visit, which had oddly turned out to be an interview, must be finished.

"No, no, please stay," Jacqueline said. "I'll get you another drink and I'll join you. Smoke if you wish. I gave it up years ago, but I understand."

As soon as she'd left the room, Theo lit a cigarette. He remained standing, wandered a bit, looked at objects without concentrating and thought about whether he wanted to get out of there as quickly as possible or stay forever. He wondered if Jacqueline could really help him. He stopped at a series of small sketches in frames on the wall, cross-sections of a church. They reminded him of charts hung in doctors' offices. Cross-sections of muscles. Diagrams of organs—heart, liver, lungs, winding intestines. The food-group pyramid with its shafts of wheat and wedges of cheese. He inhaled deeply. It was a delicious cigarette.

When Jacqueline came back, she set down a tray of drinks on the desk, went over to the wall to the left and pulled back the curtains. The window behind was in fact a set of doors that opened onto a small patio enclosed by tall cedar hedges and concealed from the front yard. There was a little round table and two chairs. Jacqueline took the tray outside and sat down.

Theo stood at the threshold. The air was fresh and he didn't recognize his own feelings. He felt conflicted. A little sad, a little hesitant, but at the same time powerful.

He sat in the perfect quiet beside Jacqueline, finishing his cigarette and starting his second large drink of the day, and Jacqueline didn't ask about where he came from or what his family was like or even about his past with Charlotte. She did ask about Curtis, and Theo told her how the two of them shared an apartment in a house near Main Street, and how Curtis worked in software. As he talked about Curtis, Theo felt slightly guilty that he was sitting here now without him, but just slightly. Maybe he should send Curtis a photo to prove that he was actually there. That would make him crazy. Lunchtime drinks in the sunshine. Jacqueline leaning in, her arm around his shoulder. *Very spring break*, Theo thought. And absurd considering how old she was.

That wasn't the real picture anyway, a party on the patio or two friends having a laugh. No. It was something else. And he wasn't quite sure what.

NINE

FROM HER BEDROOM window Charlotte watched Theo walk down the driveway and out of sight. She was clutching the curtains, cursing. *She* should have been the one to sit and talk with him, not Jacqueline. *She* should have greeted him. *She* should have been there.

Charlotte dropped the curtains. Someone was in the hallway. There was a quick double knock. Jacqueline pushed the door open but didn't come in.

"Why wouldn't you see him?" she asked.

Charlotte thought about it, wondering where to begin.

"It's about that man, isn't it?" Jacqueline said. "His father. Are you going to let that man keep you in your room?" Jacqueline kept spitting the word *man*, and Charlotte didn't know what to say. There were too many questions, too fast.

"You said you wanted to see the boy." Jacqueline said it like an accusation and waited with her hand on the doorknob, but Charlotte couldn't bring herself to answer. "By the way, I told him you were sleeping."

As the door clicked shut, Charlotte let out her breath, bowed her head and cursed again. Cursed herself for hiding in her room. She did want to see Theo. More than anything. But the idea of seeing him with Jacqueline there, in the middle, muddying things ... She stopped pacing. She hadn't realized she was pacing. She sat down on the end of the bed. She didn't know what to do with herself.

Maybe she didn't have to do anything. Maybe she had it all wrong. Maybe Theo didn't want answers. And she didn't have to explain or apologize or try to make sense of the past or remember the chain of events. Maybe she didn't have to tell the story.

Jacqueline's car started in the driveway. Charlotte went to the window and watched it pull away. She wondered where Theo was now, already up the hill, already on a bus. She had the urge to run down the driveway and up the street. She imagined stopping at the top, looking left, right, and seeing nothing, nothing but cars. No Theo.

But she couldn't do it. She couldn't go up the street. She couldn't go beyond the driveway. Not anymore. In the beginning she'd just been so grateful to have someone take care of her. But now ... She didn't know what she was afraid of.

When did I become a coward? she thought and put her feet into the white satin slippers beside her bed.

She opened the door and listened for sounds in the house she knew weren't there, went silently to the landing and down the stairs, half-expecting Jacqueline to jump out from around a corner. She couldn't shake it, this feeling of being the punch line to somebody else's joke, the clueless rabbit pulled from a hat.

In the kitchen she put on the kettle, wondering if Theo would come back.

She wondered if he remembered the last time they had seen each other. She certainly did, his last words traced on her back. She counted the years. Thirteen. It was thirteen years ago. She had known it would be their final time together. Johann had planned it that way, sending Theo off to a friend's for the night to make the disappearing act seamless. Johann would pick him up the next day and drive off forever, all the dirty work done in the night. Charlotte had begged him to find another way, insisting that Theo have the opportunity to say goodbye. It was only fair. *What will you tell him when you pick him up?* she had asked. *How will you explain?* Johann was beyond explaining.

Charlotte and Theo were sitting on the living room floor, playing that game where one person traces letters with their finger on the back of the other person, who in turn tries to guess the words that are spelled. Theo was writing something on Charlotte's back, and he'd gotten as far as *you are a kookoo* ... when he'd jumped up, yelled goodbye and run out the door to join Johann, who was calling from the front hall.

Goodbye.

Charlotte remembered staying there on the floor until her legs were stiff and her shoulders and chest ached from crying. She had stayed there until all the tears were gone, and when she stood up, she was a dry thing, walking around knowing that Johann was in the house again, packing— what couldn't fit in the car would be picked up by a moving company in a couple days, and there was an envelope on the kitchen counter with rent for two months. In the morning he was gone and Charlotte was horrified to find that the tears had filled up overnight and she had to cry them out all over again. Over and over. And she agonized over the fact that she couldn't separate the tears, the ones for Theo and the ones for Johann. They shouldn't touch.

They came from different places and here they were all mixed up like dirty dishwater.

The water in the kettle boiled, pulling Charlotte back to the present. As she poured it steaming into the teapot, she imagined an act of alchemy that could separate the tears, the impure from the pure, the betrayal from the loss, a mad science more direct, more practical than any psychotherapy, tiny bottles green and brown with little cork stoppers lining the shelves of the medicine cabinet, bottles marked *cruel*, *innocent*, *wasted*, *lost*, *found*.

She took her tea to the piano and leafed though some music Olivier had left for her. Standard stuff. She was hoping for something new. She lifted the lid to the keyboard and played a few notes with one hand. She wished she could really play.

Johann had been wrong. She should have said goodbye.

TEN

THE FIRST THING Charlotte said to Theo when she opened the front door was: "I wasn't sleeping yesterday when you were here."

"Alright," he said and followed her into the large room where the party had taken place.

It was quiet, altered. The piano was there at the foot of the stairs, the lid closed. The doors to the terrace were closed too. And the big, round table, which had stood just where Theo stood now, was pushed off to the side against a wall. There were two white sofas, facing each other. And a glass coffee table between. It was here that Charlotte stopped. She went around one side of the table, Theo the other, and they both sat down. Theo picked up a deck of cards and started to shuffle.

"You weren't sleeping," he said after a moment.

"No."

They laughed.

"I'm glad you came back," Charlotte said.

"Yeah, well, I'm a sucker for suspense and a stiff drink."

Theo dealt the cards and put the deck face down in the middle. Charlotte didn't have to ask what they were playing. Rummy was an old favourite. She'd taught him how to play.

"Jacqueline doesn't like cards. She says it's for the proletariat," Charlotte said.

"I thought it was what aristocrats liked to do when they had nothing to do. You know, parlour games and all that, summers in the country."

Charlotte looked at the cards in her hand, the spades lining themselves up one after the other.

"And a fox hunt," Theo said. "You need a good fox hunt, right?"

Charlotte looked out the window, thinking about the coyote. "I'd like to see a fox," she said. There were no foxes in Vancouver. Coyotes, raccoons, but no foxes.

Before long, Charlotte had two runs of three ready to go down but she was holding out for the six of spades to link them all together in one long, pretty row, three through nine. Over her cards, she watched Theo. He was quite beautiful, this young man she didn't know, yet did. His hands were beautiful, broad but not square, long fingers that worked the cards smoothly, holding them in perfect balance. *It's remarkable how cards just fit*, she thought. They fit into hands so naturally, nesting there, sliding back and forth under the thumbs. Charlotte's two thumbs met, leaning in like secretive souls over the nine of spades.

"It's your turn," Theo said.

"Is it?" Charlotte looked up. "Do you remember 52-Card Pickup?"

"Yeah."

"That day ..."

"The day it poured cards? Yeah, I remember that day. How many decks did we use? Like, ten or something?"

"Something like that," Charlotte said. "And we had

to sort them all out afterwards, and a couple of them went down the heating duct. Your father was not impressed."

"No, he wasn't."

"He didn't laugh. I thought eventually he would laugh."

"He did not laugh."

"You know," Charlotte said, looking at her cards again, "I hadn't thought about him in a long time until you showed up."

"Yeah, sorry about that."

Charlotte left it there. She didn't want to drag Theo into the past. He was here, now. They were playing cards. It was her turn. And that's what mattered.

She drew from the deck, discarded her lone heart, laid down her string of spades, and sat back.

"You didn't say *rummy*," Theo said.

"Rummy."

Olivier came in from the kitchen. He clapped his hands together once. "So, the lady would like to know if Theo will be joining us for dinner this evening, and the lady would like to know if the two of you might like an *apéritif*."

"Hell yes!" Theo said.

***

They had been called to dinner. Theo carried his glass of wine into the dining room, considering the doors. *There sure are a lot of doors in the house*, he thought. This one leading to the dining room was unassuming, just a door, but he eyed it as he passed through. Then the fresh air hit him. More doors! Like the ones in Jacqueline's office, they opened to the outside onto a concealed patio at the front of the house. Theo looked out, taking it all in—the little table and chairs, the cedar hedge. It was almost identical.

"You can sit here, beside me."

Theo turned to see Charlotte standing at the dining table, smiling, her hands on the back of a chair. And beyond her—another door.

In this house, Theo often had the feeling that he was trying to keep up, catch up, that he was one little step behind. And now, in this moment of staring down the door behind Charlotte, he felt just one little step in front.

Draw, he whispered. The door swung open, and Olivier came in with soup, followed by Jacqueline, with more soup. And the dinner began.

They dipped their spoons in steady silence, the taste of summer, green and fresh, and for Theo, who was used to the pulse of things, the speed and shout, it was new, unsettling, this silent soup.

Once it was finished, Jacqueline began to talk about Theo's portfolio. Charlotte cleared dishes. Wine was poured, another course served, polite questions asked about Curtis and Grigore. They talked about the food, and Jacqueline confessed that she didn't cook much these days, and Theo confessed that he didn't cook much more than noodles from a package, and he complimented Jacqueline on the meal. They asked about the restaurant where he worked, and he avoided the questions as best he could, and they didn't seem to mind but poured more wine.

Again Theo imagined the snapshot he would send to Curtis, perhaps Jacqueline sitting tall in her chair, Charlotte and Olivier standing behind, and behind the three of them the Chinese lacquer panels on the wall. Formal, out of place, out of time. Like that picture from *Butch Cassidy and the Sundance Kid*, the portrait. Butch is sitting in the front. Sundance and the girl are standing in the back. And Theo always thought there was something not quite right about it, like it covered too much ground or got hung up somewhere like a lost time machine, somewhere between the Wild West and 1970. He asked if any of them knew the film. They all said no.

"You know, Robert Redford, Paul Newman. You must have seen it."

They said no, they hadn't seen it.

"Wait," said Charlotte. "I remember now. The bike. I liked the part with the bike."

"Yeah, it's good that part with the bike," Theo said.

"It always reminded me of another movie that had a bit with a bike, a Woody Allen movie," she said.

"Really?" Theo racked his brain. "You don't mean the one with the flying bike, do you? Where they're all running around in the woods? What is that one … I know it, I know it …"

"I don't think that's the one," Charlotte said.

"That one's not so good," Theo said.

"Are any of them good?" Jacqueline asked bluntly.

At first Theo wondered if this was Jacqueline's way of changing the subject, but she kept talking about it, and Theo couldn't believe it when she finally announced that she'd never even seen a single Woody Allen film.

"However," Jacqueline said, "I've heard there's a new one set in Paris."

"Yes, there is," Theo said, settling back in his chair, glass in hand. "And that one, in fact, does have a bike."

"Of course it does," Jacqueline said, raising her glass in his direction. "It's Paris."

And so she and Olivier told them about bikes in Paris and how the ladies would ride in skirts and heels, and the men in suits, and nobody with a helmet, and how it was all so beautiful. They kept talking about Paris, and Theo stopped listening to the actual words and watched the talking, the polite intimacy, and Charlotte too, beside him, smiling as she traced her finger in the last sweet bit of sauce on her plate and put it in her mouth. *It was beautiful*, Theo thought. All of it.

ELEVEN

THEO WAS PISSED off. He had been perfectly content sitting on the white sofa drinking his *digestif*. To be chucked out into the night when the night was so young—it just seemed wrong. And this bus, so painfully slow and bright, kept picking up people that Theo just didn't want to look at. The idea of a bike was starting to seem pretty damned good. Summer was here. He should get a bike.

He closed his eyes and leaned against the window. The cold glass was comforting, and with his hand on his forehead, he could block out most of the light. But then someone sat down next to him with a bunch of bags, forcing him to sit up and shift over. He looked at the lady incredulously, but she stared straight ahead, pretending not to be seen. His phone buzzed. It was Curtis, letting him know that they were all still at the bar if he wanted to drop by. Excellent. He wasn't ready to go home.

He stretched out his legs and let his knees fall open, expecting the lady to move when his knee touched hers, but there was nothing, no twitch, no huff, no nothing. She just stared straight ahead. They stayed like this until Theo's stop, each exercising the precise amount of resistance to hold their position, awkward and hostile.

Theo shook it off and walked the half block to the bar. He ran into Kenji coming out and asked him for a smoke, but Kenji had quit. Right, he'd forgotten that. When were they going to play tennis again? Kenji said he'd call.

The rest of them were sitting in the back, and when Theo approached the table, everybody but Curtis cheered. Theo reached out to him, palms open.

"Seriously?" Curtis said. "The prodigal son?"

"Come on!" Theo yelled. "Who's buying me a drink?"

Again there was a cheer and someone motioned to the server.

"Theo's been busy," Curtis said, "spending quality time with his sugar-mumsy."

"No, no, no," Theo said, shaking his head. "There's no sugar in this gig. And are you talking about Jacqueline? She's fucking eighty years old."

"She's sixty, she's stylish, and she's loaded. And, she has a real mommy for Theo too."

Theo didn't respond. While everyone else went back to their conversations, he ordered a beer, pulled over a chair and squeezed in next to Curtis.

"What are you talking about *real mommy*?" Theo asked, keeping his voice low.

"Isn't that what you're always telling me, you never had a mother?"

Curtis was right—he did say that. His mother had died when he was a baby, and he never really knew her. Had no memory of her. So whenever there was talk about mothers, he always said he didn't have one. But it was one thing for *him* to say it, another thing for someone else.

"Come on, it's obvious," Curtis said. "After all these

years, you've finally found a mother. Not only that, you have a grandmother who can cook for you and give you pocket money."

"Hilarious," Theo said.

But Curtis kept going, talking about the mother Theo never had and the father he took for granted. It was insane. He kept spitting out words, and Theo sat back and crossed his arms and stared, barely believing what he was hearing and thinking it would all just come to an end. But it didn't. It kept going. And it stung. And the more it stung, the harder Theo looked Curtis in the eye, wondering what the hell had come over him. And then, through all of Curtis's hiss and sputter, Theo saw it. Right in front of him. He leaned forward onto his elbow.

"Are you wearing a fucking beret?" he asked.

Curtis stopped and lifted his chin.

"Yes, I am. Do you like it?"

"No, I don't like it at all. It looks like shit. You should take it off."

"I won't take it off. I like it. Now stop abusing me and tell me what you had for dinner."

So they went out front to smoke, and Theo told Curtis everything he wanted to know—how the table was set, what they ate, what they talked about, what Olivier was like, the stories of Paris.

"You have to get me another invitation," Curtis said.

The night went on, and occasionally Curtis would ask about a detail or make a joke about Theo's *new friends*, which struck Theo as odd because Charlotte was really the oldest friend he had. He kept ordering drinks on Curtis' tab and bumming cigarettes. And at one point he found himself sitting next to a girl named Leah, whom he'd never met before. She kept putting her hand on his arm when she talked, so he started paying attention to her. She was really quite pretty. She told Curtis that she liked his beret.

"No way," Theo said.

And this set off a little argument between Theo and Leah, which Curtis watched, amused and vindicated in his beret. And Theo didn't have to move closer to Leah because she had already moved closer to him and would sometimes put her hand on his chest when she talked now. The three of them decided to go. Theo just wanted to have one more smoke before they left, so he went out back and smoked some weed with a couple of friends, and when he came back, Leah was gone.

"You always have to push it just a bit too far, don't you?" Curtis said.

They started home, the two of them, walking a route they'd walked a hundred times together.

"Maybe if I had a beret, she would've stayed," Theo said, snatching Curtis' hat and putting it on his own head, laughing. Curtis stayed quiet. Once they got home, he put two cigarettes on the kitchen table and said good night.

Theo was alone now. He wavered, looked around. He didn't like being left, and he wasn't finished talking. He'd meant to tell Curtis about the beautiful part, about the beautiful way things could be. He just didn't know how to put it so that it didn't sound stupid.

He picked up the two cigarettes and put the beret on the table in their place. He went to his room, opened the window and climbed onto the sill. There wasn't far to fall if he fell, but he didn't. He stayed balanced, anchored to

the moon, a moon so big and white that it absorbed every
little thing that came into his head — Leah, the bus, the
bikes, his father, his mother, the beauty. He let it all go, let
the moon have it.

TWELVE

CHARLOTTE WONDERED HOW long it would take to run out of air. She was breathing so quickly, and the sheet didn't rise and fall with each breath as she expected but stayed settled over the contours of her face in just the way she had dropped it, draping at the high points—her brow, her nose. It was soft, the cotton, and as she focused on this, her breathing slowed. She calmed and soon realized that she would not run out of air, not gasp for breath, not die like this.

And in the calm, she noticed the heat. She opened her mouth and breathed out more heat. *Lovers' heat*, she thought. And she was surprised that she could see through the sheet. From the outside, it looked opaque, but from the inside, resting on her eyelashes, with the light coming through, it was translucent. She could see the ceiling, the fan, the window, the walls. *In between*, she thought. *I'm in between*. Neither inside her body nor outside the sheet, she was in between, with her breath, an in-between breath.

She listened to the sound of the piano downstairs, a familiar tune but too far away to place. The doorbell rang and the music stopped. She listened to the sound of Olivier walking to the front hall and opening the door. Talking. The door closing. Theo! Theo was here. She swept the sheet off her face and swung her feet into slippers. As she stood up, she met herself in the mirror, too naked. She pulled a dress from the closet, buttoning the bodice as she went downstairs.

There was no one in the living room. Charlotte heard voices coming from Jacqueline's office down the hall. *Everyone must be there*, she thought. *I'll wait for them here.* She rested her hand on the piano and raised one foot like a flamingo. Her slipper fell off and smacked the floor. She put it back on and looked at the music that Olivier had been playing. Of course. It was the old Nina Simone, *Tomorrow is My Turn.* A spider had spun a web between the open lid and the prop and sat in the centre of it. Charlotte watched it, black and waiting. Olivier emerged from the hall.

"Still fighting with the Nina?" he asked.

"I wouldn't dare fight with the Nina," she said. "Did you know there's a spider here?"

"Yes, indeed. She has been busy all morning. I haven't the heart to move her. But one thing we do not want is a hundred baby spiders launching their life in our piano. That happened to me once in a car. They must have hatched somewhere under the hood, and when I started the engine, they all came pouring out of the dashboard. I had to flee. There were waves of them."

When Olivier started to play, the web shivered. Charlotte stared at it. Olivier kept repeating the opening bars, waiting.

Charlotte plucked the first words of the song, tugged at the notes. Theo came into the room, smiling. He was carrying a large, yellow envelope, and when he sat down, the envelope slipped from his hand and smacked the floor just like Charlotte's slipper had done. She glanced at the headshot that slid out. Theo bent over to pick up the bits, and Charlotte continued to pick at the music, draw it out, dig.

Jacqueline walked in and went directly to the back of the room. She lifted a large vase of wilting flowers and carried it off to the kitchen. Almost immediately she was back at the table where the flowers had been, looking at the fallen blossoms and leaves. She turned her attention to the windows that ran the length of the south wall, determining whether the marks were on the inside or the outside.

Theo decided he should stay put so that he wouldn't make any more noise. He watched Jacqueline inspect the windows, the bookshelves, the tables, moving from object to object without a sound. He was fascinated by her feet, soft and silent, her steps following the pulse of the piano. It was hypnotic, the music.

But Charlotte felt unsettled. She kept chipping away at the song. Then she realized she was doing the exact thing she'd told Olivier she wouldn't dare to do—fight. She didn't want to fight. So she eased off. She found her breath, felt her weight in it, inhabited it, and before long found herself back beneath the bed sheet and the in-between, where she could still see, where in hiding she was free to reveal, where death was visible, where breath was life. She was so focused that she didn't notice that she'd stopped singing.

Olivier withdrew his fingers from the keys and folded his hands in his lap.

It took three seconds before the silence reached Charlotte. Theo was watching her, concerned.

"It's awful, isn't it?" Charlotte whispered.

"No," Olivier said. "In fact, the opposite."

"But it's predictable. Nostalgic. Circles. I keep going in circles."

Olivier looked hard at her.

"It is rather morose for such an optimistic song," Jacqueline said from the other side of the room. "And why," she asked, looking under a lampshade, "are there so many spider webs today?"

Olivier stood up and addressed Jacqueline in an un-characteristically buoyant voice. "There are spiders to catch your flies." And he left.

Theo wanted to tell Charlotte how amazing the song was, but he knew that's not what she wanted to hear. She wanted the song to be different somehow, and Theo had no idea how. It was one of those things where you didn't know what it looked like until you saw it, and as he was thinking about this, he remembered his father shouting. First he was shouting about something Theo couldn't re-member, and Charlotte was pleading *you don't under-stand,* and his father was pleading back *make me under-stand.* Make me understand. What can a person say to that?

Jacqueline sighed and walked over to the piano, put her slender arm around Charlotte's shoulder. "Perhaps you are right, *ma chérie.* Perhaps the song is tired. But I am confident you will come up with something."

"For what?" Charlotte asked.

"For Saturday. Theo, please invite your friend. And darling, we must discuss the dress. But before Saturday, there is tonight. We have company. I've got to call Joy back to clean this place. And did you hear the news? Theo has an agent. We must celebrate. Let's have fun, yes?"

And with that, she exited.

Charlotte and Theo were left turning it over in their heads—the fun—regarding it from this unlikely, sunken room, where eight hours later they were expected to rise to the occasion.

Theo was in a bit of a stew, reconciling his moods. He didn't like being told what to do. But the invitation for Curtis was good news. And the yellow envelope in front of him was excellent news. As he recognized his good fortune, he warmed to the idea of a party, and in his mind tasted his first drink, leaned casually on the piano and saluted Olivier. Before long he had cast himself in a suitable role. He was bound to have fun.

Charlotte was imagining the evening too. She saw herself sitting halfway up the stairs, watching everybody else. Maybe there was someone she wanted to dance with. She hadn't danced with anyone in a long time.

She looked now at the web on the piano. The spider was gone. She scanned the strings but didn't see it there. She looked at Theo. He was looking at his phone.

"I wonder who's coming tonight," she said.

THIRTEEN

THEO WOKE UP with the image of Elise in his head compounding the problem of his current hard-on, which was only a problem because of an overwhelming need to piss. It's disturbing waking up not knowing where you are. There's a period, sometimes just a split second, sometimes longer, where you're lost, truly lost. But this morning Theo woke up knowing exactly where he was —upstairs in Jacqueline's house in a guest room—knowing exactly how he'd got there. He smiled at the fact that Elise had snuck out while he was still asleep.

And he remembered the time he'd woken up on the floor in a house he'd never seen before and had no idea how he'd got there. People were sleeping everywhere, tangled, askew, and as he made his way downstairs and through the house, he looked at each face and didn't recognize a single one. And since there was no one he knew to recount the story, the story itself was lost. But this story, the story of last night, was all there—Elise taking the drink from his hand and shutting him up.

Theo thought about it now, trying to ignore the other problem, the one aside from the piss and the hard-on, and that was the problem of the water. He was dead thirsty, and the jug of water was all the way across the room on the table, and this bed was the most comfortable bed he'd ever slept in, and he had no ambition of leaving it. If it wasn't for the fact that he really, really had to urinate, he would have opted to delay the water in favour of staying in bed to jerk off. As he pulled on his jeans, he wondered who would wash the sheets. Must be Joy.

Five minutes later, Theo poured a glass of water, drank it, poured another. He was standing at the table, looking out the window, thinking about Charlotte and Jacqueline, if it was all okay that he had stayed there with Elise. He figured it must be. Jacqueline had told him which room he could sleep in if it got too late, and no one seemed to care what was going on, not even Elise's mother, who had come with a whole bunch of European dress samples.

Elise wanted nothing to do with it, the impromptu fashion show. She said she was bored of it all. Her mother pointed out that Elise was wearing a dress from the collection, a dress which Theo pointed out to himself was made of silk and moved in an exceptional way each time she uncrossed and re-crossed her legs. She seemed older than the girls he knew, but she said she was only twenty-one. There were two men with moustaches who could have been twins, and they stood alongside Olivier, the three of them occasionally watching the women model a new outfit but more interested in their own conversation.

Charlotte preferred to perch on the stairs. She told Theo that she liked watching everyone instead of everyone watching her. She said that sometimes other musicians came and performed and then she was really happy. She and Olivier played around with some tunes. Eventually Theo sat next to Elise on the sofa instead of across from her.

What an excellent night, Theo thought, staring now

at the tops of the trees and the tops of the roofs to the east. The sun was already quite high. He picked up his phone to check the time, but it was out of power. He tossed it back onto the table. The ashtray there was empty. He checked his pockets for the third time since getting dressed. Still no cigarettes. He looked around the room. No clock. He picked up his phone again, knowing that it would still be out of power, but unwilling to accept the fact. What if someone was trying to get hold of him? Curtis was probably worried because he hadn't come home or answered his messages, which were sure to be there.

Theo didn't like this feeling of being cut off. Anything could be happening out there in the world, and he'd have no idea. He'd never seen a TV in the house, just the laptop in Jacqueline's office. What if there was a catastrophe? A natural disaster? A terrorist attack? He'd have no way of knowing.

He looked around the room again. No phone either. He opened the closet door. It was empty except for some clothes on hangers and a pair of shiny shoes below. *Those are some ugly fucking shoes*, he thought. He pulled one of them out with his toe and put his foot in. It fit. He took it off and looked at the size. Yup, that was his size. He put it back, lined it up next to the other shoe, and an awful thought came to him. He eyed the clothes hanging in front of him—three shirts and a tuxedo. Was it possible that these clothes were meant for him? No, that was crazy. What was he thinking? He pulled open the first drawer. Socks and boxers, brand new. He slammed it shut and opened the second drawer. A couple T-shirts and a pair of jeans. He held up the jeans, and as they were unfolding in front of him, there was a knock at the door. He threw them down. "Come in."

It was Jacqueline. She stepped into the room and looked at the jeans on the floor.

"I guessed your size," she said.

"You guessed right."

"There's nothing worse than putting on last night's clothes."

Theo didn't say anything, didn't flinch, just looked Jacqueline coolly in the eye.

"I'd like to know how the tuxedo fits," she said. "But you can try it on later. You might want to take a shower. There's a bathroom next door, and you should find everything you need there. If there's anything you are missing, just let me know. In case it has not been made clear, you are welcome to stay here." She held out an envelope. "This is for your friend, an invitation for Saturday. I don't have one for you as you are practically family now."

Theo had to step forward to take the invitation. He turned it over in his hand—the same heavy paper as before, the same handwriting spelling out Curtis' name.

He stood waiting for Jacqueline to leave, but she wasn't leaving, she was staring past him. He moved out of the way, letting her go by, and she sat down on the edge of the bed, facing the window.

"I like this room," she said. "It gets the morning sun. It used to be my office when my husband was still alive. After he died, I took over his office downstairs. It's much more practical."

This was the first Theo had heard about a husband. He'd always just imagined Jacqueline without one.

"They keep telling us that we have arrived," she said, still staring out the window. "That we've finally become a big, grown-up city."

Theo didn't know what she was talking about. He was trying to keep up—the tuxedo, the room, the invitation, and this idea of a husband—he couldn't help but wonder, in all the talk about rooms, which room the husband had died in. Or had he died there at all?

"Do you know what the problem is?" Jacqueline said. "Sawdust."

Theo frowned. What was she talking about?

"This whole region was built on coal and forests and I don't know what else, but when I first came here, that's all there was. Sawdust, beer, hockey. I despised it."

She looked at Theo when she said this, and Theo frowned harder. He had the impression she was accusing him, lumping him in with the sawdust and beer, and at the same time assuming that he would agree with her, that he would agree what a horrible thing it all was. It was just like his dad. His dad did that. He'd throw down insults, so matter-of-fact, without even realizing they were insults, and just expect Theo to agree. It was crazy. Why would he always agree?

"I quickly realized something," Jacqueline said, looking out the window again. "I didn't have to get used to it. I didn't have to adapt. I didn't have to settle for less. I could shape my own world, cultivate it, fill it with all the things that I loved."

"Well, I like hockey!" Theo blurted out.

Jacqueline tilted her head in his direction, raised her eyebrows. Suddenly he felt stupid and wished he hadn't said anything. He was still holding Curtis' invitation, gripping it between his knuckle and thumb. He threw it into the closet like a Frisbee and grabbed the jeans off the floor, the ones that Jacqueline had bought, and threw them in too. He stormed past her to the far side of the bed, found the shirt he'd been wearing the night before and yanked it over his head. It had been such a great night, and now he was in a bad mood.

He stood with his hands on his hips, not knowing where to go.

Jacqueline didn't say anything. He expected her to, but she didn't. She turned away calmly. He followed her gaze toward the sunlit window and breathed deeply. It occurred to him that Jacqueline must have stared out that window for a lot of her life. *That's a long time to be in one place with one view*, he thought.

Dust danced in the light, and the light washed her out like an overexposed photograph, smoothing her skin, revealing tiny tendrils of hair usually tucked out of sight. She was sitting exactly where Theo had been sleeping, and he thought again about Elise, and how Jacqueline was resting her hand on the sheets, and how it didn't matter. There were too many pointless boundaries in this world that just didn't matter. And what did it matter if she wanted to create her own little world? *What a strange little world*, he thought. *And I'm in it.*

FOURTEEN

NOBODY WAS TALKING about the weather. They were talking about flowers and menus and music. *My Funny Valentine* was on the program, and outside on the terrace Olivier was telling Theo about Berlin when he was nineteen and how he left his friend to the mad parties and took a train back to Paris, sitting beside a German girl going to Paris for the first time. She sang *My Funny Valentine* to him in a whisper. She said she wanted to get it out of her head. It was making it hard for her to sleep. She hoped that, if she sang it to someone, it would go away.

"Did it?" Theo asked.

"I don't know. We said goodbye at the station."

Theo contemplated the story. He pictured the German girl striding out of the station, confident and cured, and Olivier at nineteen, watching her go, melancholy and wearing a rumpled version of the same custom shirt he wore now.

"The problem is," Olivier said, "I've had to carry around that song ever since." He flicked a ladybug from his sleeve. Theo watched it open its wings and make a rudimentary flight down, landing on pot of dahlias. It was a long way to Berlin.

Theo put out his cigarette. He could hear Jacqueline talking to someone inside. She'd been talking non-stop all day. He tried not to listen and sensed that Olivier was trying to do the same thing.

"She's upset," Olivier said. "She won't admit it, but she doesn't want me to leave. I go back to France on Tuesday to spend the summer with my daughter."

Theo processed this new information, all the while listening to the sound of Jacqueline's voice coming from inside. She was far enough away that he couldn't make out the actual words, but close enough that he couldn't ignore her either.

Whatever she was talking about, whatever anyone was talking about, nobody was talking about the fact that it hadn't rained in a week. Nobody was talking about how blue the sky was, how perfectly blue and cloudless it was, or how the days were heating up and soon the nights would too. The heat had risen to the second floor, and windows were opened to create cross-drafts, letting in the cool air off the ocean. The city took to the beaches, stripping off layers of Gore-Tex, ugly false skins, and marching forward, a sun-thirsty zombie. And at Jacqueline's house, cotton was being pressed, white cotton and linen.

Upstairs, Charlotte was having a good inch snipped off her long hair. The ends fell from the hairdresser's scissors, some of them resting in the creases of Charlotte's cape, and when there was a pause in the snipping, Charlotte would push them with her hand from underneath the cape, sending them sliding down onto the bathroom floor, where they gathered in little heaps, animal-like, a squirrel's tail, a rat. She thought about a heap made of all her hair if all her hair was cut off. It might amount to a raccoon.

Theo looked in, and the hairdresser asked if he'd like a shave.

"No," he answered immediately. "No thank you."

He walked away, disturbed. No one had ever offered him a shave before. He ran his hand over his cheek, his chin. He didn't need a shave anyway.

Charlotte was soon back in her room, her eyes on her hair, swept up and pinned, her mind on the Nina Simone song and what she had found there, that sensation of being in between places, or states. She wanted it back. She wanted more. She knew there was more. Her face was pale, cameo, unwavering, but inside she was a riot, too rowdy to move. How could she move without it all coming out?

She plotted her steps away from her reflection to ensure she wouldn't trip. She didn't want to unravel. She didn't want to burst open. That was not what was required. Containment was required. And so she sat near the window like a queen in crinolines, dismissing the obvious, superfluous thing that was her *self*. She wished she could put it aside. Remove herself so that what was left was all that was left. *I have to remove myself. That's it. That's what's required. I'm in the way.*

"I didn't know Olivier was leaving." It was Theo, standing in the doorway. Her eyes welled at the sound of his voice. She was caught off guard by the emotion but stayed contained.

"He goes every summer," she said.

"How old is his daughter?"

"I don't know. A few years younger than me, I think. Maybe thirty-five, thirty-six. You know he has grandchildren."

Theo sat down on the end of the bed but got right back up and went to the window. He struggled with the latch.

"No, not that one," Charlotte said. "There's a wasp out there that gets very angry every time I open the window."

"You should get rid of it. Spray it or something."

Theo went over to the other window, which was already open, and pushed it out as far as it would go. It made no difference. The air was stagnant. He stared at the empty patch of ground below, then at the tall cedar straight in front of him, marked by a crow, watchful.

He went back to the bed and sat down, checked his phone. Nothing from Curtis. Theo had dropped by the house while Curtis was at work and left the invitation on the kitchen table. He'd sent a couple of messages too. But no response.

"Are you worried he won't understand?" Charlotte asked.

"Who?"

"Curtis."

"Yeah, I guess. It's just, I'm kind of leaving him stranded, you know."

Charlotte wanted to tell Theo that he didn't have to live here at the house, but she knew that in a way, he did. She wanted to tell him not to think in absolutes, that it didn't have to be one way or the other, but she wasn't convinced. She was struggling with this idea herself—the idea of the absolute, the pure, the essential. She was greedy for it. And suspicious of balance. It seemed a lovely trick—balance— at odds with the concentration growing inside her, this feeling of intensity, of saturation, as though the quieter she got, the more complete she became, the more true.

Theo cradled his blank phone in both hands. Charlotte wanted to give him some words of encouragement, but not her tangled mess of thoughts.

"It's funny," she finally said. "It's funny how things come full circle, isn't it? It sure feels like home with you here."

Theo looked up. Nobody had ever said anything like that to him.

FIFTEEN

IF CURTIS DECIDED to show, Theo wanted to be right there. He hung back in the spot where he'd stood after Jacqueline had welcomed him that very first night, watching her now shake hands and kiss cheeks in the same seamless manner. From here he could see the guests arrive but didn't have to bother with introductions. Every time someone glanced his way, he flashed them a smile, and they smiled back. He didn't recognize most of them. They streamed in with the warm air. A large ceiling fan spun stealthily overhead. Jacqueline had set up more fans throughout the house. There was a collective vibration. Theo felt it in his bones. He wanted a drink but he'd wait. If Curtis was going to come, he wouldn't be late. Curtis hated being late.

Theo felt a bit guilty being on this side of the door while Curtis was still on the other. It had been Curtis' idea in the first place, coming here. Curtis' vision. Theo hadn't meant to take it over, hadn't meant to cut him out. It had just happened. Charlotte had happened. Then the agent. And the dinners. And all the rest—the time, the freedom of time, the flow of it, the flow of all sorts of things, music, Elise, afternoons. Theo loitered in the shadow of Madame Jacqueline Day, comfortable in his new role. The tuxedo was a perfect fit.

There he was, walking toward Jacqueline, handing her

a little wrapped gift. He was dressed impeccably. He even looked like he'd been in the sun. Jacqueline kissed him once on each cheek and passed him to Theo, who grabbed his hand, embraced him, and was on the verge of pouring out a bunch of stuff about the suntan, James Bond, text messages, but instead led him out, passing behind Jacqueline, noticing that she had placed the little wrapped gift on the tall hall table with the red dragon legs.

They went straight out to the terrace, where a whirring fan drew a crowd and kept the mosquitoes at bay. The sun was going down. White lanterns dotted the garden. Theo handed Curtis a glass of champagne.

"To summer," he said, raising his glass.

"Where's your girl?" Curtis asked.

"There is no girl."

"To summer then."

Theo offered Curtis a cigarette, took one for himself and lit them both. Curtis accepted without comment but raised an eyebrow as Theo put the pack back in his jacket.

Theo explained about Elise, how it had been just that one night, very cool, no plans, she wasn't even there at the party. Curtis made a joke about the gazebo not being there either, and Theo accused him of watching too many musicals. Curtis said that he couldn't stand musicals. Except for *Blue Hawaii*. Did that count as a musical?

"Never seen it," Theo said. "Is it hot? In the movie, is it hot?" He watched the cigarette smoke drift away from the direction of the fan to fuse with the darkening sky.

"It doesn't seem that hot. But they do have their shirts off a lot. You know, Elvis and the boys. So I guess it must be pretty warm. I've been thinking of going somewhere like that. Somewhere warm. Maybe not Hawaii. Maybe Singapore. If I could get a job there."

Theo frowned. Curtis had never talked about going anywhere before.

"You want something stronger?" Theo asked.

"Sure."

Theo asked one of the servers for a couple of gin and tonics, extra cold. It was too hot for a jacket, but he kept it on. *Vanity*, he thought. *I'm so fucking boring.*

"Sometimes I get really sick of myself," he said to Curtis. "I'm like Self, do something. Fucking do something."

"Like pay your rent?" Curtis looked down as soon as he'd said it.

Theo looked down too, right at his shiny new shoes. "Yeah, man, sorry about that. It's coming. I've got an audition next week and another one in the works. It's coming. And if you have to rent out the room, I totally understand."

But Curtis wanted to know about the cigarettes and the clothes and how Theo could think that it was okay to spend his money on all that but not pay his rent.

"Shit, no. No, you got it wrong. They're gifts. All gifts. Even the smokes. I'm broke. I swear. I'm flat broke."

"The restaurant?"

"Done."

"Done?"

"Done. It wasn't working out."

"It wasn't working out?"

"What are you, my fucking dad? They fired me, okay?"

"Why?"

"I wasn't really showing up enough."

Curtis dropped his head forward. It seemed like he was struggling for words. A little round tray was thrust between them, two glittering glasses, lime and ice, beading in the heat.

"Fine," he said, raising a glass. "To summer then."

The cold liquid set everything right.

"Come on," Theo said. "Let's go see Charlotte."

***

The door to Charlotte's room was closed. Theo knocked.

"Are you sure this is a good idea?" Curtis whispered.

"Of course. She wants to see you."

Charlotte stood facing the north window, the wasp window, the one that stayed closed. She wore a long, sleeveless gown embroidered with glass beads, amber, bronze, black and green, a scene of pyramids and palm trees. Motionless, elegant, she shrank the room, and a fan blew hot air nowhere. Theo took off his jacket.

"How does a sundial work?" Charlotte asked, not turning from the window.

Theo looked to Curtis for help.

"Well," Curtis said, "basically there's a stick, and depending on where the sun is in the sky, the stick will cast a shadow. And the position of the shadow tells us what time it is. At least I think that's how it works."

There was no sun. It had set. There was light from the front of the house and the driveway and the streetlamp in the distance, and Charlotte watched people pool in the light, follow it, laugh, hold hands, adjust a belt, a strap, a tie.

"You know," Curtis said, "there is such a thing as a moon dial."

Charlotte turned around. She held out her hand to Curtis.

"I'm glad you came," she said.

"Look over here." Theo was leaning out the west window. "There's your moon."

When Charlotte approached, the pyramids and palm trees on her gown caught the light of the moon and came alive. Charlotte drew back her hands as though her fingers might get burned, and they all watched.

Theo sat on the floor below the window and lit a cigarette. He passed the pack to Curtis.

"Do you mind?" Curtis asked Charlotte, as he took one out.

"No, I don't mind." Charlotte swayed ever so slightly. The smallest movement set the light in motion. After a while Charlotte took a step backwards, out of the moonlight, and the beads started to fade, turn away, settle down. It didn't happen all at once like a light switching off. As Charlotte retreated, she left traces, traces of fireworks suspended with the smoke after the bang, phosphorescence, glimpses of fish scales fleeting in the deep.

Theo watched, resting his glass on a bent knee. Curtis was leaning on the window sill.

"It's nice and quiet here," Theo said after a bit.

"Since when do you like nice and quiet?" Curtis asked.

"Since sometimes."

"What are they like, down there?" Charlotte asked. "Did you happen to meet a man named Patrice?"

"No," Theo said, "Who is he?"

"Jacqueline's latest ambition for me. Watch out, Curtis. She'll be setting you up with someone too if you're not careful."

"I can use all the help I can get," he said, and they all laughed.

Then they were quiet again, the three of them complicit in their isolation.

"I never had a dress like this when I played the clubs," Charlotte said. "It was more of a sequins scene. Lots of drag. God, I was young. They called me Little Sister. I'd forgotten that. Always wanted to dress me up, lend me things. Borrowing and lending, that's what we did back then. Nothing to lose that way."

Theo liked this idea—nothing to lose. It was such a waste of energy worrying about what there was to lose. He always tried to let things go. Toss them away. Even the things he had to offer, the things he wanted to give. *Here— this is what I've got—if you want it, take it—if you don't, don't.* That was his philosophy. "If you worry about what there is to lose," he said, "you never do anything."

Charlotte and Curtis both regarded him.

"It seems like another life, the sequins," Charlotte said.

She focused again on the wasp window and Theo looked at the wedge of lime in his glass. The ice cubes had melted to nothing. It was time to go. He put on his jacket and checked himself in the mirror. He and Curtis wished Charlotte a good performance. Theo touched her arm gently, and she nodded. Curtis bowed slightly as they left the room.

"Somehow I get the feeling we weren't talking about

sequins anymore," Curtis whispered on the other side of the door.

"Did you just bow in there? Where do you come up with this shit, man? And moon dials? Holy fuck! I'm glad you're here. You're not going to try some crazy stunt like sliding down the banister now, are you?"

"Are you kidding me? I'd break my neck. Now, where do we refill these things?"

They ambled down the stairs, empty glasses in hand.

* * *

Charlotte lowered the black scarf over her head. The silk fell in folds across her face, and the tassels met in front, an arrow headed for the centre of the earth. Her gown, half-hidden, sparkled still, but sombre, in darker hues, in baser things, rooted and ancient. The impression in the mirror was a little grim, a little widowed. But it was exactly what was required. A vein in her neck pulsed, but nobody would see. She was faceless, anonymous.

She put her hand on the banister for a second to steady herself, then let go. *Does nobody see me?* she wondered, feeling each stair with the back of her heel.

But they did see her. One by one, people turned their heads, and by the time Charlotte had reached the last stair, a hush had spread across the room.

"Why is she wearing a veil?" Curtis whispered to Theo.

"No idea."

Theo noticed Jacqueline weaving her way out of the crowd to the far side. She turned around. She didn't look pleased.

He turned too. Charlotte was standing by the piano now. Shrouded. Dark. Regal. They all waited.

Charlotte could feel the waiting. Ripples of light filtered in through the silk. She closed her eyes, breathed slowly. *I'm the only one who's breathing*, she thought. Notes from the piano rolled out, one over the other, connected, continuous, and with them—her voice.

There were words. Regular words. But the words were just shells, and they fell away without recognition. Discarded ciphers. Points on a panel of crumbling code. They fell. They fell away so that anything that meant anything was in the sound.

She'd done it. She'd reduced everything to its essential form, if only for the length of a song.

Olivier lifted his hands from the final keys and looked up at Charlotte. There was a moment, then the crowd burst into applause.

Theo felt a hand on his shoulder.

"Are you okay?" Curtis whispered.

Theo wasn't clapping. The ice cubes in his glass were shaking. For a second he thought there must be an earthquake, but then he realized it was him. He was the one who was shaking. And the vibrations of his own body were merging with the clapping and the shifting of feet and the whirring of fans. He felt dizzy, but Curtis left his hand on his shoulder, and it helped. And where normally there would be shouts of *encore!* there was an unspoken request for the removal of the veil. They all wanted to see Charlotte's face. But Charlotte didn't move. Theo wanted to rush up and shield her from the crowd.

Why? Why would I do that? he asked himself. *They're clapping. They adore her.*

Something in the music had moved him in a way that he didn't understand, shaken something loose.

He stared at the place where he thought Charlotte's eyes must be, beneath the cloth. A rhythm was building in the crowd, an internal chant. It grew, and pushed, and Theo felt like he was going in the wrong direction, pushing back against it, and while the room was entreating Charlotte to show her face, he was willing her to *run, run, run, run*.

Jacqueline stepped from the shadows and pulled the veil free. The beads on Charlotte's dress threw hundreds of tiny stars. The applause surged.

Charlotte's eyes blinked into the fact of the performance. She smiled, curtsied, stretched out her arm to acknowledge Olivier and received Jacqueline's kisses gracefully. Theo thought he saw her arm pinched tight as Jacqueline led her away.

* * *

Theo was waiting for Curtis in the southwest corner of the garden. He was on his second cigarette and his drink was done. Finally Curtis showed up with a refill. Olivier was with him. The three men clinked glasses.

"Unbelievable," Olivier said after a moment. "Was it just me, or was that ... remarkably different?"

Theo looked hard at him. "No, it wasn't just you."

"I've never ... I've never quite heard her like that. Or anyone. Ever. Anywhere." Olivier punctuated each statement with a flick of his wrist, sending ash into the garden. "And such a little song." He looked down at his shoes.

Theo looked down at his own shoes, unsure of what to say.

"Do you know what she told me?" Olivier asked. "Earlier this evening. Before the performance. Before the veil, which I didn't know about by the way." He was getting louder. "She said: *Don't worry. I know you have to go away. It's okay. I do too.*" He threw his cigarette down on a paving stone and crushed it with his foot. "What does that mean?" A few guests up on the terrace turned to see what the noise was about. Olivier lowered his voice. "Where would she go?"

They drank in silence, the three of them. Theo wished he had something to say, something to offer Olivier, some wise words, a joint, a joke, the answer, any answer, but it seemed impossible to articulate how something so beautiful could make you feel so uneasy, and sad. At least, that's how *he* felt. He wished he had a joint for himself. Or a girl standing next to him. He could put his arm around her waist.

He didn't know what to make of Charlotte's words. Like Olivier said: *Where would she go?*

Theo gave his last cigarette to Curtis, crumpled up the empty package, tossed it up and batted it away into the dark with a clenched fist. It made an unsatisfactory brush of a sound as it hit the grass somewhere.

Curtis then produced his own full pack of cigarettes and held it out to Theo. He'd been holding out all along.

"You bastard," Theo said, laughing. "Do you know what I'm going to do?" He slapped his hand down on Curtis' shoulder and leaned in. "I'm going to build you a fucking gazebo right in the middle of the lawn." His eyes blazed with the thought of it. He wavered a bit, took a step back, fumbled for his lighter.

"Olivier, when you come back," Theo said, gesturing towards the yard, "it'll be right there, all shiny and white."

"Don't hold your breath," Curtis said to Olivier. "Theo never finishes anything."

"Where's the faith?" Theo said. "Where's the faith? Olivier, I swear, when you get back, you can have your fucking tea in that gazebo."

SIXTEEN

THEO WAITED WITH Margot for her taxi. Her hair was spectacularly red. The front door was wide open, but they stayed inside, the high sun too much for last night's cocktail dress. Margot was rummaging in her purse. The shouting upstairs started again, and she snapped her purse shut and glanced at Theo. He kissed her, and that drowned out the sound for a moment. He wanted to go back to bed, rewind, but the taxi pulled up the long drive. They kissed one more time.

Theo closed the door, leaned against it. The shouting had stopped. He'd never heard Jacqueline shout until that day.

On his way back through the living room, he paused, looked around. He hadn't noticed it when he'd come down with Margot earlier, but the room was immaculate, everything in its place as though the night before had never happened. It was incredible.

He looked out to the terrace, piecing together the events. The backyard looked smaller in the daylight. He remembered the gazebo and smiled. He started up the stairs.

"I prefer that they don't sleep in," came a voice. Theo looked up. It was Jacqueline, on the landing, in a black kimono. "Bad form."

"Bad form," Theo muttered.

How did she do that? Appear out of nowhere. Like a cat.

Theo dreaded the idea of walking up the stairs past her, but he was already on his way. He could make an excuse, go to the kitchen, or outside. If he had a smoke, he'd go for a smoke, but his hands were empty. And he wasn't wearing a shirt.

No, he thought, *I can do this*. He chuckled to himself and continued his way up the stairs. The moment he moved, Jacqueline turned her back on him and walked away.

"When you're dressed," her voice called out as he reached the landing, "go and see Charlotte."

Theo didn't get dressed right away. He took a long shower. Then he replied to a couple of messages from Curtis, who had gone home at about two o'clock in the morning. It had been a good night. Olivier was drawn back to the piano and played without his usual restraint—hungrily, slap-happily, the music spilling out like from a ragtime saloon into the night air begging to cool down. Margot appeared out of nowhere, a houseguest of someone. Theo was astonished by the colour of her hair and tried to take a picture of her, but she ducked out of it. Among several shots of blurred streaks, one photo captured her running from the frame, looking back, laughing, the camera flash making her white skin even whiter. Theo looked at it now, wishing she was still there.

He deleted the photos and stretched out on the bed, his hands behind his head.

When he knocked on Charlotte's door later on, there was no answer. He went downstairs. There was no one in the living room. He stood by the open terrace doors a moment, listening. Finally he found Charlotte in the kitchen making coffee. She made some for him too and they carried their cups out, but Charlotte stopped Theo at the open doors. She wanted to stay inside. So they sat in their usual places on the white sofas.

"Everybody's out," she said.

"I've never heard her yell like that."

"She didn't like the veil."

"Is that what she said?"

"Not exactly. She said that performance art was dead."

"But it was good. What you did was really good. Isn't that all that matters?"

Charlotte wondered if this was true. It had felt good. It had felt right, pure, direct. But that's not what Jacqueline had seen.

"She said she didn't bring me here for that." Charlotte looked down when she said it. The statement sat there, like a stone, between them.

They drank their coffee, and after a while, Charlotte picked up the deck of cards and started to shuffle.

"People are surprising sometimes," she said. "Last night after I sang, Jacqueline introduced me to the man named Patrice, the one I was worried about, remember? She left me alone with him, and he said to me: *Don't worry, you don't have to make small talk with me.* Maybe he didn't feel like talking himself, but the thing was he knew that I didn't want to talk. He stood beside me while people came and went, shaking my hand, saying the things they say. He stood there the whole time. Some people looked at him inquisitively, but he never said a word to them, and I never introduced him. He put his arm around my shoulder at one point. He was very tall. And when the stream of people finally stopped, he let me go."

There was the sound of a key in the front door. Charlotte and Theo lowered their heads and concentrated, not on the cards in their hands but on the space between them, the stone, the statement, the man named Patrice who had stood there.

Olivier came into the room.

"So I'm staying another week," he said. "One last hurrah."

SEVENTEEN

THEO GOT A job. That was one of the things that happened during the week. He landed a small role on an episode of a local cop show, playing a street kid sitting on the sidewalk with his dog. It was formula. Two cops showed him a picture of a girl, he said *never seen her before*, they said *let us know if you do*, he said *sure thing*, they said *and get that dog of yours a leash*. He was scheduled to film on Friday.

It may have been formula, but for Theo, it was huge. It was his first professional spot, and it was a speaking role, exactly what his *résumé* needed. He called Curtis as soon as he found out.

"Friday night," Theo said. "Drinks at the usual. Are you in?"

Curtis was in.

Another thing that happened during the week was the tennis. Kenji wanted to meet up, but Theo didn't want to go all the way to Curtis' to get his racket. He asked Jacqueline if she had one, and she told him to look in the garage.

Theo had never been in the garage. It was separate from the house, on the west side of the front yard, and hardly used, even for the car. He walked across a patch of gravel to the side door. The handle turned easily. He went in. It was stuffy. He had expected it to be cooler inside, but it wasn't. He flicked on a light switch.

There was a big empty space, and a few dried-up oil patches on the cement floor. There was a snow shovel just inside the door, and a bag of road salt. There were old garden tools hung neatly, and a couple of extension cords coiled up on hooks. Along the back wall was a workbench with a big clamp screwed to it. There were cans of paint and varnish and a plastic milk crate full of rags. There was an axe, a couple handsaws, tool kits stacked one on top of the other, screwdrivers, pliers, files and paintbrushes all gathered in coffee tins, a level, a measuring tape, and a row of jam jars filled with nails and screws and other bits of hardware. There were garden torches, a croquet set and three old bikes—two ten-speeds and a city bike with a basket in the front. Theo checked the tires—they were all flat. There were some cobwebs here and there, but otherwise things were clean and organized. There were fishing rods, a large pair of gumboots, and two tall stools that looked like they'd come out of an ice-cream parlour. And there was an empty birdcage.

The tennis rackets were hung on two nails. Theo took one down and turned it in his hand. No cracks. The grip seemed fine. He bounced the strings on the palm of his hand. They seemed okay. There was a can of tennis balls. He took it off the shelf and opened the lid. The chemical smell escaped after decades. The balls were grey. He put them back on the shelf.

Theo walked back to the house, bouncing the old racket off his forehead. Charlotte was in the living room, looking through one of Jacqueline's art books.

"Look what I found," Theo said.

Charlotte put the book down at Rauschenberg.

"Do you remember?" he asked.

She leaned her head to one side.

"Tennis," he said. "You and my dad. You used to play. I used to be the ball boy."

"Me? Are you sure that was me?"

She had an image in her mind, but it was unclear. And static. Stuck like a half-done Polaroid. She stared hard at the image, but it didn't evolve, didn't get any clearer. Again she doubted the reliability of her own memory.

Theo stood there with the racket, spinning the handle in half-turns, half-looking at the book on the coffee table, the all-white canvasses whiter than the paper they were printed on, and Charlotte, following Theo's line of sight to the open pages and following the motion of the racket, feeling its rhythm, saw that what was there was as concrete as a thing could be—a page, a book, a racket. But even these concrete things were not fixed. They moved. They faded. They cracked. The racket spun. The right page of the book, buoyed by the breeze from the open doors, might turn.

And Charlotte wondered why she would expect anything different from her memories. Their accuracy, their certainty, maybe weren't that important, maybe not even possible. *The paintings in the book—they aren't fixed either*, she thought. They were reproductions of something that had already happened. But there they were, there to see, reflecting sunlight each time the right page caught the breeze. Charlotte watched the page bob up and down and listened to the sound of the racket in Theo's hand, a slight brush on each turn, and in the all-white, in the sunlight, she heard laughter, her own, and saw Theo running after a ball. She walked up to the net to pick up a ball there. Johann met her from the other side and reached across to touch her. She leaned over the net and kissed him.

"Yes, I remember," she said.

* * *

After half an hour of tennis, Theo needed a break. It was hot, and he was out of breath.

"I smoke way too much," he said. "I've got to cut down."

"So what's the deal?" Kenji asked. "Are you living up at that house permanently now?"

"I don't know about permanently, but yeah, I'm living there. It's pretty sweet."

"Isn't it kind of boring? I hardly see you out anymore."

"No, it's not boring. There's stuff going on, it's just different. And the parties, like, man, it's a whole other world."

"Money?"

"Sure, there's money, but not crazy money. Not like those parties you used to take us to when you were dating Amy. That was insane. Kids with way too much cash. This is different. It's ... how do I explain? It sounds pretentious, but *cultured* maybe? Like she's on the opera board and is always going to fundraisers and shit. But you got to remember, these people are old."

"Two ladies, right? Curtis told me."

"Right. Two ladies. And this guy Olivier too. He's cool."

"And now you."

"And now me."

As Theo said it out loud, he realized how strange it

sounded, the situation. He didn't mention to Kenji that one of the ladies was someone he used to know. Really, really well. He didn't want to get into all that. But maybe Curtis had told Kenji that too.

"It's weird," Theo said.

"It's all weird, man." Kenji got up and started collecting tennis balls. "The modern family. We're fucked. I'm pulled in so many different directions I don't know where I am most of the time." He tossed one of the balls to Theo, who was still sitting on the asphalt. It bounced off his shoulder and rolled onto the court. "Let's play."

***

Another thing that happened that week was the arrival of Francisco and Mimi. When Theo came back from filming on Friday afternoon, they were sitting on the white sofa in his spot, drinking tea and reading the newspaper. They greeted Theo like a long-lost nephew and insisted that he eat some cookies. They were from Argentina, friends of Jacqueline, and they were on their way to the Rocky Mountains.

"We're taking a train," they said.

Theo invited them out to the terrace. They surveyed the garden, the three of them, and Theo felt like a proud old man. He wanted to tell them about the gazebo he was planning to build but felt a bit stupid. They asked about the local wildlife, so he told them about the coyotes and raccoons, the skunks and squirrels. They wanted to know if they would see a bear. He said it was highly unlikely, although there were bears on the North Shore and not long ago one of them hitched a ride in the back of a garbage truck and made it all the way downtown before the driver noticed it in his rear-view mirror. It was in the news. Then they talked about the Rocky Mountains and the bears they might see there, and the moose. They were excited about the moose.

By the time Jacqueline and Olivier came back to the house, things were flowing. Francisco had poured the first drinks of the evening. Charlotte had come downstairs. And Theo was excited about the night.

Jacqueline made a toast to Francisco and Mimi and their upcoming adventure, a toast to Olivier and his trip home, and a toast to Theo, to his recent success and the beginning of a great career.

"To journeys," Jacqueline said. And they all drank.

Charlotte tipped the glass to her lips, felt the cool bubbles run over her tongue, the taste nutty and rich, not at all like the cheap stuff that they used to blast open at the club, that would greet her the next day, dried up and sick-smelling and mingled with Obsession and Angel and Chanel No 5.

EIGHTEEN

THE TAXI SAILED through green lights and quiet streets with no lights, where people didn't sit on their front stoop to enjoy the warm evening but set up barbecues in backyards, hidden from view. Theo kept looking from his phone to the road, occasionally leaning forward to get a better view of what was ahead, as though that might speed things up. He was supposed to have met Curtis an hour ago. He shouldn't have had that last drink. But they kept pressuring him to stay, and then when Jacqueline offered to pay for a cab so that he didn't have to take the bus, he couldn't say no.

Still no word from Curtis.

The taxi turned south onto Main Street, and the look of things changed—greasy spoons and Chinese imports, the legion, the liquor store, McDonald's and vegan, vinyl records and indie fashion, antique furniture, modern furniture, thrift shops, coffee, typewriters, more coffee, paper lanterns, aprons printed with pink roses, real roses and orchids, stitched-together kitsch and noodle houses, the old and the new jumbled together, unpolished except for the odd bit of 1960s chrome caught in the headlights. Wherever there was a restaurant patio, there was a crowd. And in between was the night sidewalk, carrying people along, people on their way to some place, or people asking for spare change, or people pushing shopping carts heaped with the contents of their life. Theo watched it all slide by.

Finally the taxi arrived. Theo paid the driver and put the change in his pocket. He went inside and found Curtis alone at a table, looking at his phone.

"Damn," Theo said, sitting in the chair across from him, "I thought you'd be partying with the usuals."

"No," Curtis mumbled. He took a sip of his beer but didn't look up.

"You would not believe how hard it was getting out of there," Theo said. "They were trying to get me to stay for dinner, setting a place for me, and I was like man, I'm already late, I'm so late, let me go." Theo was looking around for a server. "There's this couple visiting. From Argentina. You'd really like them. Super nice people. They're going to the Rocky Mountains on Monday."

Curtis put his phone on the table and pushed it aside. He looked up and sighed. He looked tired. Theo asked him if he'd ever been to the Rocky Mountains.

"Sure," Curtis said. "When I was a kid. We stayed in Banff. Then we drove to Calgary to go to the Stampede. I got a cowboy hat."

On another day, it would've been a funny story. On another day, Curtis would've said more about the hat. But today he didn't. He raised his glass to make a toast but put it back down. "I guess we need to order you a drink," he said. The two boys looked over to the bar, but no one was paying attention.

"I'll go," Theo said. "You want another?"

"Sure," Curtis said.

Theo came back. "They're on their way," he said.

Curtis was looking at his phone again. Theo took his out. The two of them waited in silence, checking their phones, for nothing.

The drinks arrived and Curtis said: "Congratulations. To fame and fortune."

It was an empty toast. Theo wasn't sure what to make of it.

"Thanks," Theo said. "Thanks, man." The beer was cold and perfect. Maybe Curtis just needed a bit of time to warm up.

"The filming yesterday," Theo said. "It was unbelievable. It was … easy. You know what I mean? When something just flows? You don't even have to think about it? Seriously, having this one gig on my résumé … it's huge."

"I'm glad it's finally paid off," Curtis said.

"Me too," Theo said, nodding his head.

"All that kissing ass has finally got you a job."

Theo sat back and half laughed. "You don't mean Jacqueline."

Curtis raised an eyebrow.

Theo looked toward the door, looked nowhere really. He was stunned.

He turned back to Curtis, picked up his pint. "What can I say, man? If that's what you think."

Curtis leaned forward. "Don't you think she's using you?"

"For what?" Theo said. "I do absolutely nothing. I sleep in. Someone does my laundry. I show up for dinner and I fucking drink all the time."

"So you're using her."

"Yeah. I guess I am."

Curtis looked down at his hands. He slid his phone to

the side again, slid it back. He did this a couple times, then looked up.

"I can't keep your room anymore," he said. "I have to rent it out."

"Right. Right. Yeah, man, of course. I totally understand."

"Taylor's going to take it."

"Taylor? Taylor who used to work at your office? I thought she irritated the hell out of you?"

"Yeah, well, she's okay. She needs a place, and I need the rent." Curtis slid his phone back and forth again then put it away in his pocket. "I need you to move your stuff out."

"Right. Shit. Where am I going to put it all?" Theo started to imagine what he'd do with it, where he'd put it, how he'd move it. Who did he know with a truck?

"This weekend," Curtis said.

"This weekend? You want me to move it this weekend? You can't be serious. How the fuck am I supposed to do that?"

"You know, I really didn't want to tell you this. All I wanted to do was meet up, have a drink. But … what am I supposed to do?"

They stared at each other for a moment.

"Fine," Theo said. "I'll come over on Sunday." He picked up his glass. "Wow. To think that I missed dinner for this."

"Well, I'll let you get back then," Curtis said, standing up.

"Hey! Where are you going?"

But Curtis didn't answer. He just left.

NINETEEN

CHARLOTTE CAUGHT SIGHT of the cyclists through the wasp window. She was half dressed. There were a lot of buttons on her blouse, and before she could finish doing them up, the cyclists were gone, down the hill, to the sea. They were Saturday cyclists. Serious cyclists. Cutting a trail through the heat, disturbing the drugged beast of midday.

The heat shifted, and a breeze from the other window drew Charlotte's attention. She did up the last button. She was thirsty for tea.

***

"Not a crowd," Jacqueline explained. "A small gathering. And dinner. We're sitting down to dinner." Jacqueline didn't take her eyes off the screen of her laptop. Charlotte fiddled with a stray paper clip, bending it halfway open and hooking it over the rim of her empty teacup.

"It will be quiet after everyone's gone," Jacqueline said. "We'll have a little break. You're tired."

Charlotte wasn't tired at all. She wasn't tired or sick or depressed or any of the things that Jacqueline kept mentioning, and she certainly didn't need a break. A break from what?

"This heat," Jacqueline said. "It's *insupportable*." She

pronounced the word in French. "All these years ... drowning in rain ... now I'm praying for it."

Charlotte wondered if Jacqueline actually prayed. It was just a figure of speech, but still, maybe she did pray. Charlotte had no idea. In the ten or more years they'd known each other, it was something they'd never talked about. They'd talked about religion in the context of politics, Jacqueline railing against any church influence in government, but they'd never talked about religion for the sake of religion, and never about their own faith, if they had any.

I pray, Charlotte said to herself. She meant to say it out loud, but it didn't come out. *I pray sometimes.*

"I thought about having dinner outside," Jacqueline said. "But I don't want to be bothered by mosquitoes. Mind you, they're not that bad right now, the mosquitoes, are they?" Her fingers tapped lightly on the keyboard. She kept her nails short and always manicured, usually painted a deep red, as they were today. "Olivier says you are singing the Nina Simone after all. I don't understand the fascination with this song."

It's beautiful. Then Charlotte said it out loud. "It's beautiful."

Jacqueline stopped typing and looked at Charlotte as though disturbed by the sound of her voice. Then she turned back to the screen.

It's beautiful, Charlotte said again to herself.

* * *

The afternoon was gaining momentum, and Charlotte sat in the middle of the activity, her back propped up against a cushion on the white sofa, her knees bent, and a book resting upside down on her chest.

Every so often Jacqueline came through, carrying something—a vase, a pile of magazines—talking as she passed, talking in all the rooms, little reminders trailing behind her, notes to self, or to Joy, who was upstairs, vacuuming, or to the chef's assistant who, earlier, had carted in crates and knives through the side door and was now making noise in the kitchen. Charlotte listened to the ringing of pans and stainless steel, the whisk, the water, the expert chopping— heavy metal on heavy wood on Jacqueline's marble countertop. She was absorbing the sounds of the house, taking them all in, drawing the energy, harnessing it, storing it. The more still she kept and the more concentrated she was, the more engaged she felt, the more potent.

The front door opened. Charlotte wondered if it was Theo, or maybe Olivier. There was a quick shuffle in the entranceway as shoes slapped the tiled floor. That had to be Theo.

He came in full of salt and sun, looking out of place against the polish and linen. He stood in front of a whirring fan and eyed the empty sofa where he usually sat.

"I need a shower," he said.

＊＊

Charlotte had never felt so good. Her dress slipped over her head. There was no resistance. Her shoes were all the way across the room but getting them didn't require effort. They didn't need to be got. The boundaries between things seemed less fixed, less obvious. Charlotte noticed the fluidity of her bare arms, saw their contours and how they moved in the air, and how the line between arm and air moved too. And it made her rethink an old image of *Swan Lake*, where the swan princess was superimposed on the stage as though the stage and curtains were a cardboard hoax, and Charlotte, in her mind now, reached in with the hand of a god to lift away the proscenium and set the dancer free.

* * *

Mr. Lourie was one of the guests. Charlotte had always liked him, his sincerity. He was an excellent pianist and had brought along one of his students who was around the same age as Theo and was making waves across the country on the classical circuit. Jacqueline asked the student if he'd play later that evening, and he said he would. His name was Jeremiah.

Francisco and Mimi were there, a few others, a lady wearing enormous red eyeglasses. Charlotte had met her before. Publishing, she remembered. Olivier had brought his glass from the dining room and set it on the piano. Francisco was opening a bottle of sparkling wine to serve with the dessert, and the publisher was teasing Jacqueline about her choice. Jacqueline said that she was trying to be progressive and that she wanted to give Francisco and Mimi a sample of the local wine. They all tasted it, except for Olivier and Charlotte, and agreed that it was really quite good. Not champagne, but really quite good.

Charlotte watched Theo and Jeremiah sitting next to each other but not talking, both in tuxedoes, Theo without a tie and still wearing a bit of the beach. Jeremiah was listening to the conversation while Theo stared out the terrace doors.

Olivier touched Charlotte's shoulder. "Are you ready?"

She stood up and followed him to the piano. There was no getting ready, no need to get ready. It was all there. Breath. Time. Already there. She listened to Olivier play, looked around, looked at the open faces in front of her. She felt the line of the song extend outward, towards them, around, and back to her, and out and back again, a loop, a circle, a circular stream. She felt a heat at the bridge of her nose and behind her eyes, a slight vibration echoing the whir of the fans, the memory of the cyclists' wheels, their spin, their spokes indistinguishable one from another, their anticipation of the hill down, the free fall. She sang the most pure, direct, complete thing she had ever sung. There was no resistance. No walls, no lines, no separation between words and music and audience and herself. Nothing was in isolation. Everything lived in the breath. She felt part of, and whole, and joy—she felt joy.

That's what Charlotte experienced.

That's not what Theo experienced.

Theo waited. He waited for Charlotte to start singing. He wondered if the silence was part of the performance, something that he just didn't get, like the veil she had worn that last time, like some kind of performance art. He looked around. The others were watching Charlotte, waiting too. It reminded him of a scene from a movie where everyone waited around a radio, waited through the crackle, waited through the dead air, waited for the speech to start, afraid that it would never come. And then it did, and everyone breathed a sigh of relief, and listened. That was in the movie. Here, they waited still. Transfixed.

Charlotte didn't look quite human. Her feet were hidden under the hem of her dress, and she seemed to rise from the ground. *Like a statue*, Theo thought. An ancient statue, pale, long, her dress the same pale as her skin, as though she was created from one single element. *But not stone*. Something fluid. Almost like an energy. There was movement there, even in her stillness. There was life. And there was light in her eyes.

Jacqueline stepped forward and took hold of Charlotte's elbow, breaking the spell. Charlotte looked at her, startled. Olivier stopped playing and folded his hands in his lap. The guests shifted.

"*Ma chérie*," Jacqueline said, "you don't have to perform tonight. It's not a problem. You're not feeling well."

She was guiding Charlotte to the foot of the stairs, one hand on her elbow, the other on her shoulder. Theo felt extremely uneasy. The gestures were there, the kind words, but they didn't ring true. *She doesn't mean it*, he thought. *She doesn't mean any of it*.

"Theo will take you upstairs," Jacqueline said. He wanted to protest, shout something out, but what? What could he possibly say? He walked over and kept his mouth shut.

"Poor thing," he heard Jacqueline say to the guests as he went up the stairs with Charlotte. "Too many parties. It's my fault. Really, it's all my fault."

TWENTY

CHARLOTTE SAT IN the chair by the wasp window. Theo went straight to the west window and lit a cigarette. He didn't sit down. He felt like he was supposed to do something, like it was up to him to make things right, when he didn't really understand what was wrong. Nothing was wrong. And yet they'd been sent upstairs like children. And Jacqueline saying it was her fault … such bullshit … she didn't think for one second it was her fault. And her voice all silvery like that … Theo wanted to smash it. And he wanted to knock off those hideous goggling glasses, those big fucking red glasses that lady was wearing. He couldn't believe he'd left his drink downstairs.

The cedar outside the window was solid black against the last light of the evening. Theo thought about the moon dial night, when Curtis was there, and how easy it had been to hang out, the three of them, removed from it all. How easy. He looked at Charlotte now.

"Are you not feeling okay?"

She smiled and shook her head no.

"Would you rather I go?" he asked. "Leave you alone?"

Again she shook her head.

"You do know they're all idiots," he said. Charlotte smiled again, and Theo laughed. "And if it was up to me, we'd listen to that song all night long. One continuous loop. I'd set myself up on the couch ... well, first I'd have to kick off piano-boy downstairs, but then ... I'd stretch out, put my feet up, and just let it roll over me. Like waves. Of course for you and Olivier, it would be quite the marathon. You'd need to stand there a really long time. But everybody who chose to stay, everybody who listened, they'd all go into a sort of trance. That's what I'd do."

Theo kicked off his shoes and lay on his back on the bed. He wanted a drink, but he didn't want to go back downstairs. He closed his eyes, chuckling to himself about the continuous loop. In less than a minute, he was asleep.

Charlotte took her shoes off too and placed them gently on the table beside her, and when she did, she heard a gasp, or almost a gasp because it wasn't audible in the usual sense but somewhere in the background, in the distance, a memory perhaps of someone gasping at the sight of shoes on a table. It was bad luck, some people said. And she heard Theo's laughter too, even though he slept now, breathing quietly, not laughing at all. They'd laughed about the song together, hadn't they? She'd laughed along with him, hadn't she?

Her shoes glowed under the green lamp on the table. It was too hot for shoes. She felt much better without them. She switched off the lamp and leaned back in the armchair.

But she hadn't laughed out loud, had she? She'd had the feeling of laughing, but she hadn't made a sound. Just like she'd had the feeling of singing. Intense feeling. So intense that it was best not to try expressing it vocally. Best not to jeopardize it, dilute it. Best to keep it intact and pure and strong.

Theo slept deeply. *Just like his father*, Charlotte thought. There were certain things Theo did that reminded her of Johann. The way he slept anywhere, anytime. The way he moved, his strength, his ease. Johann had been like that, but slightly more controlled, more reserved. Theo was impulsive. He just *did*. He did things because the inclination was there and it felt good. Charlotte remembered watching him sleep when he was little. Late, after work, when the house was quiet, the streets too. Or when they first moved in and Theo would ask her to tuck him in, and she'd sing softly to him, and in a minute or two he'd be asleep. She'd forgotten that until now. She'd forgotten so many things.

There was music downstairs. The piano. She listened. It wasn't Olivier. Maybe it was the young man, Jeremiah. She opened the door. The sound swelled. This was real sound. She looked back at Theo. He was fast asleep. She left the room and sat on the landing. No one downstairs would be able to see her unless they moved directly to the foot of the stairs. And no one did. Charlotte expected Jacqueline to come up, but she didn't. No one came up. Charlotte listened to Jeremiah from the landing. He played superbly. And she was grateful for the silence in her mouth that made room for the sound in her head.

TWENTY-ONE

CURTIS WASN'T HOME when Theo and Kenji showed up. They went through the front hall and the living room. Things looked pretty much the same, but tidier. And the hardwood shone.

"Come on," Theo said. "Let's get the stuff."

Everything in Theo's bedroom had been left as it was, except that Curtis had put a few cardboard boxes in the room to help with the packing along with a pile of items on the dresser he'd collected from around the house— cigarette lighters, headphones, an apron from work, massage oil, birthday cards and a harmonica. Theo picked up the harmonica and played a string of melancholy notes then chucked it into one of the cardboard boxes. He picked up the box and swept the rest of the pile in. He and Kenji looked at what was left.

There was a dresser, a futon on a wooden frame, and a chair. There were clothes lying around, a towel, the bed sheets, the towels that served as curtains, and one pillow. There were more clothes in the closet, along with a bunch of shoes, Theo's tennis racket, a suitcase, a football, boxes and bags of old papers and photographs, some books and scripts and his winter coat. Theo started stuffing things into the boxes, and Kenji followed suit.

"What's this?" Kenji asked, holding up a brown, ceramic mug.

"Oktoberfest."

"You know, you could throw some of this junk out."

"Later."

Once they had everything packed and heaped in the middle of the room, they stepped back and assessed the situation.

"It's not going to fit." Kenji said. "I told you it wasn't going to fit."

"Here." Theo took hold of one end of the futon frame. "Grab the other end."

When they got the frame out to the car and it was clear that it was too wide, they set it down on the brown, dry grass. Kenji suggested taking it apart, but Theo wanted to get the mattress first. So they half-dragged, half-rolled the futon out and dumped it on top of the frame.

"Let's get the dresser," Theo said.

They tried loading the dresser into the trunk of the car, but it was just too long, even on an angle. They put the back seats down and tried getting it in through the door, but it wouldn't fit. Finally they set it down on the grass next to the futon.

"What do I need a dresser for?" Theo asked.

He went back inside and got a big garbage bag. He dumped the contents of the drawers into the bag and tied it up. This got thrown into Kenji's car with the rest of the bags and boxes. Other than the things he had at Jacqueline's, and the furniture on the grass, this was all he owned, and it seemed like too much.

"I don't think that futon's going in," Kenji said.

"I think you're right."

They slammed the back doors shut, closed the trunk, and looked at the furniture.

"We'll just leave it," Theo said.

"Just leave it like this? On the side of the road?"

"Sure. Someone will take it."

Kenji suggested they put a sign on it that said Free Stuff. Theo said it wasn't necessary.

"At least put the drawers in properly," Kenji said, fumbling the drawers into their slots.

Theo went back to check if they'd missed anything. There were a few scraps of paper and some paper clips on the floor of his room, a poster of *Reservoir Dogs*, and a lot of dust. He considered cleaning it up but he was tired now, and Kenji was waiting outside. So he left it. On his way out he took a look in Curtis' room. There was no dust there. Nothing out of order. There were pictures on one wall, in neat rows, in black frames. And there were throw cushions on the bed. *Fucking throw cushions*, Theo said to himself.

That made him smile and gave him an idea. He went into the kitchen and opened the fridge to grab a couple beers. After all, it was moving day. But there weren't any. Not even in the vegetable crisper. There were carrots, broccoli and a big bunch of kale, but no beer. He closed the fridge door and wrote a text message to Curtis: *Where's the fucking beer?* But he didn't press send. He couldn't. It was like he'd lost the right to send whatever stupid thought came into his head. He deleted the message and left, putting his key through the mail slot as Curtis had asked.

***

After they unloaded the car and put all of Theo's things into the garage at Jacqueline's, Theo asked Kenji if he wanted to grab a drink. But Kenji had to go. He had a family dinner.

"Oh, I wanted to ask you," Theo said, "*you* know bikes, right? Those bikes over there ..." Theo pointed to the old ten speeds stacked in the corner. "Think you could help me fix one of them up? I want to get mobile."

Kenji stared at him a moment, then walked out. He opened his car door and looked back at Theo.

"West Tenth," he said. "I think there's a place there. Or take it up to campus. They'll be able to help you out."

Theo watched him drive away. Then he looked at the sun and thought about going to the beach, but maybe it was too late, and he didn't really feel like it anyway. Jacqueline's car wasn't in the driveway. Maybe she had taken Olivier to the airport. The Argentinians were gone too. He could take one of the bikes to the store to get new tires but he'd have to wheel it the whole way. At least Kenji could've offered him a ride. He closed the garage door and headed toward the house.

He looked up at Charlotte's window but couldn't see her. He wondered what she was doing. And he remembered last night, how he'd fallen asleep on the bed and woken up in the early, early morning and crept out of the room past Charlotte sleeping in the chair. And before that, the strange song. Silent. And Jacqueline shepherding them upstairs.

Charlotte's window was dark, in the shadows. Theo stopped, looking up for wasps. Where were the wasps? Were there any? Were there ever any? There was nothing there. He couldn't see anything. And then just as he was about to look away, he saw it—a tiny, grey nest tucked in under the eave at the top of the window. He had expected something bigger.

TWENTY-TWO

CHARLOTTE WAS LISTENING. To everything. She heard Kenji's car door slam shut. She heard him drive away and she sensed Theo's discontent. She heard Theo walk across the gravel, stop for a few moments, then start again. She heard him come in the front door and kick off his shoes. Go to the kitchen. Open the fridge. Take out a bottle of beer. Drawer. Bottle opener. Cap. Bottle opener. Drawer. Living room. Terrace doors. She heard him sigh and imagined him stretching at the same time.

She heard the rattle of a crow in the backyard. Then the caw of a crow down the street. And the caw of another in reply. She heard the crows in her old neighbourhood congregating in the park. She heard the crow outside the club where she used to sing.

She heard the big door that used to open into the back alley from the club. She heard the click of the big metal bar that you needed to press to open the door from the inside. And the secret knock that you needed to get back in. She heard the gossip and the raunchy jokes that circulated during smoke breaks. And she heard Danny Girl shrieking in the alley and throwing whatever object she could get her hands on, throwing it at the club door — bottles, rocks, car bits, tin cans, milk crates, even her stilettos — the night she heard that St. Francis had died. AIDS.

There weren't supposed to be any more funerals. They were so *passé*. But Charlotte went to a few in those days, wearing purple and blue and red because everyone just wanted to keep living. She heard eulogies with passages from Shakespeare and Oscar Wilde.

She heard St. Francis sing *If You're Going to San Francisco* only weeks before he died. And she heard Danny Girl sing *Danny Boy* and bring the house down every time. She heard Sid clapping his hands together. *Ladies, ladies, it's showtime. Get your lashes out of your asses.* She heard the new girls whisper about her: *What's she doing here?* She heard the older queens speak up on her behalf.

Charlotte heard Jacqueline pull into the driveway. She heard her get out of the car and walk up the front steps. Door open. Door close. Hallway. Keys. Hallway. Office. Hallway. Living room. Terrace. Talking to Theo. Too far away to hear the words. Hallway. Office. Why didn't she come upstairs?

Charlotte heard Sid's words to her: *I'm so sorry, baby. They just want something different now.* Six months later she heard that the club had closed to make way for a karaoke bar. She heard that Sid was in the hospital. Too many pills. Then she heard that he got out. She heard the rattle of her own pills when she first came to live with Jacqueline. Stabilizers. The rattle of stabilizers.

She was waiting for Jacqueline to come upstairs. She heard Theo going back to the kitchen. Fridge. Beer. Drawer. Opener. Cap. Opener. Drawer. Front hall. Shoes. Door. Door. He was gone. She heard him walk away. Then it was quiet. *It's just business, baby*, she heard Sid say. And then it was quiet.

She heard Jacqueline go into the kitchen and open a cupboard. She heard something heavy on the counter. The lid of a jar opening. Cupboard. Plate. Pouring from the jar. Not a plate. Bowl. Microwave open. Bowl. Close. Beep. Whir. Beep, beep, beep. Door. Bowl. Door. Drawer. Spoon. Drawer. Stool. Jacqueline was eating soup. She was probably starting a soup diet. It would last three days. When Charlotte concentrated hard enough, she could smell the cabbage.

***

In the middle of the night, Charlotte was the one in the kitchen. Her own sounds filled her head now. She didn't have to speak to make sound. Kettle. Water. Stove. Cupboard. Plate. Drawer. Knife. Board. Bread. Kettle whistling. Teapot. Water. Sink. Cupboard. Box of teabags. Water. The knife slicing the bread. Charlotte heard a cough upstairs. Theo. She had heard him come in late and bang his way to bed with gestures that were meant to be stealthy but weren't. Now he coughed in his sleep. When she concentrated hard enough, she could smell pot and carbon dioxide and the sea.

Charlotte poured the tea. The sound of it streaming into the mug was one of the most beautiful sounds she'd ever heard.

She never used to hear Johann coming home at night. She was usually the one out late. But she heard him in the morning. The shower. She'd drift back to sleep. Then the hangers in the closet. Sometimes she'd drift back to sleep again. If not, she'd hear Theo getting into his chair at the kitchen table and pouring cereal into a bowl. She heard Johann making coffee and Theo's lunch, talking to Theo, asking him questions about school. Theo didn't say much in the mornings, even then. Sometimes she'd slide back to sleep again. Johann would kiss her before he left. In the beginning at least. Then she would hear the shoes and coats and doors. There sure were a lot of doors to hear.

TWENTY-THREE

THEO SAT UP and drank the half-glass of water beside his bed. It was a bit warm. He looked at his phone. 11:05. *Not late at all*, he thought. Good, he had plans for the day. Well, not exactly plans, but ambitions. Now that the weekend was behind him—the move, the goodbyes, the strange Saturday night—now that it was all out of the way, he could focus on getting things together. He looked at his email, but there was nothing interesting. He'd kind of hoped that there would be something from Curtis, at least acknowledging that he'd cleared out the room.

Theo's arm was crazy itchy. He looked down where he was scratching and saw three swollen mosquito bites in a row. Then he remembered the night before, drinking at the beach with the Mexicans. There were lots of Japanese and Mexican kids in town these days, learning English. They liked to party, especially the Mexicans. He remembered that someone had a ukulele. Curtis would've got a kick out of that. But Curtis didn't like the beach. Too much sand.

Theo pulled on his jeans and went into the hallway. The house was quiet. The door to Charlotte's room was closed. Jacqueline's too. The hall window was open but there was no breeze. Theo looked out onto the driveway and saw that Jacqueline's car was there. She must be home.

He thought about knocking on Charlotte's door, but she might be sleeping. He looked again at Jacqueline's car. He should start with the bike. Today. That's what he should do—start by getting one of those bikes fixed. Maybe if he mentioned it to Jacqueline, she'd offer to take it to the shop. Maybe. He could bring up the subject, see what she said.

He was halfway down the stairs when he heard his name. Was that Jacqueline calling from her office?

"I'm in here," she called out.

Damn, Theo said under his breath. Why did she have to do that? It was like sneaking up on a person. He thought about turning around and going back up, but he was caught. There was nothing he could do but go down. And when he got there and stood in the doorway of Jacqueline's office, he didn't feel like talking about the bike anymore.

Jacqueline gave him one of those up and down looks, and he realized that he'd pretty much rolled right out of bed and down the stairs but who fucking cared anyway, other than Jacqueline, except now that he thought about it, he wouldn't mind brushing his teeth.

"Theo, are you happy here?" Jacqueline asked.

It was one of those questions. One of those set-up questions. How was a person supposed to answer a question like that? And the way she said *happy* with no *h* and *here* with no *h*—it was hard to take seriously. *Am I appy ear?* Theo asked himself.

"Yes," he answered.

"Good. I want you to be happy," Jacqueline said, standing up. "You know, that's all I want. That people are happy."

Theo slid his tongue back and forth over his teeth and wondered where this was going.

"Charlotte is not happy," Jacqueline said. "So you see we have a problem."

She placed her hands squarely on the edge of the desk and leaned into them. It was a boss kind of thing to do, a man boss kind of thing, and it reminded him of the first time he'd been in that room and how it had felt like an interview. Now, weeks later, it still felt like that. Then one side of Jacqueline's blouse fell open, and Theo didn't even pretend to look away, and Jacqueline didn't pretend either.

It was high noon, and every Western Theo had seen rushed into his head—every dusty Main Street, every sun in the sky, every tumbleweed, every squinty eye. But then Jacqueline relaxed her arms and stood up straight, her blouse falling closed into place, and it was over. She came around the side of the desk and held out her hands to him. Theo felt his stomach tighten. What now? What was she doing? Did she want him to come into the room? He stood in the doorway with his arms crossed. She wanted him to come in and take her hands, didn't she? *Fine, I'll play your game.*

He went in and put his two hands in hers, and she folded her slender fingers over his, and the feeling wasn't bad at all. That was the surprising thing. Her hands were warm and smooth, and it felt okay.

The two of them stayed like that for maybe two seconds, then Jacqueline let go and asked about Charlotte. She wanted to know what Charlotte had told him, what Charlotte was thinking, feeling, what was wrong. Theo didn't know. He explained that Charlotte didn't talk to him, they just hung out together. Jacqueline didn't believe him, but Theo insisted. "She hasn't said anything about anything. She hasn't spoken a word, literally."

Jacqueline looked at him curiously, processing what he was saying, turning it over in her mind. He could tell that this was news to her.

"You mean she isn't talking at all?" Jacqueline asked.

"That's exactly what I mean. And you know what else, I think she *is* happy."

Jacqueline let out a little puff of sound, a short little *ha*, as she turned to the patio doors and flung them open. But there was no rush of air. The air was stuck, and Jacqueline was stuck there with it. Theo had the impression she might seize up, self-combust like he'd imagined numerous times before. She seemed so brittle and volatile, and the thing that confused him the most was that while she stood there with her back to him now, so inhuman, he felt the lingering warmth of her hands holding his.

"Don't worry," Jacqueline said. "We'll figure it out. We'll help her." She turned around, perfectly calm, as though she'd been calm all along. "You will help her."

They both nodded their heads, just slightly, down and up, in unison, unconscious of the action. Theo was afraid to speak.

Jacqueline picked up an envelope from her desk and handed it to him. "This came for you today."

It was his paycheque. From the acting job. He wondered if she wanted him to open it right away, but he just held onto it. He said thanks then lingered because Jacqueline usually had one more thing to say. But she went back to her computer screen, so he left.

It wasn't until he had reached the kitchen that he felt that the conversation was safely over. He ripped open the envelope and stared at his first acting cheque. $964. Not bad. Then there'd be residuals. And he had another audition coming up, for a commercial. The first thing he had to do was pay his cell phone bill. After that he could pay Curtis. But before paying Curtis, he'd get one of the bikes fixed. It shouldn't cost too much. He'd wheel it up to the shop later on. But first maybe he should celebrate, go get breakfast or something, treat himself to breakfast. Or lunch. It was pretty much time for lunch. He could find a patio. Maybe he could take the bike in, then have a beer on a patio while he waited for it to be fixed. He was too hungry to wait. He made some toast and ate it standing up. He wondered about Charlotte. He was still hungry, so he made more toast.

TWENTY-FOUR

THEO PUSHED THE old 10-speed up the hill. He'd chosen the burgundy one. The day was already too hot. He wondered if he should have seen Charlotte before leaving. He wondered if there was actually something wrong.

The bike didn't roll very well with its loose, slappy tires. Theo tried carrying it for a bit, propped up on his shoulder, but that was even harder, so he went back to pushing. Something didn't add up. Jacqueline said she wanted to help Charlotte, but Theo just didn't see it. There was something off about her concern. It seemed reluctant, almost resentful. It was too bad that Olivier was gone. Maybe he could have helped.

The hill flattened out for the last block. Theo arrived at the bank and stuck the bike in a rack. He didn't suppose anyone would bother stealing it.

He took the paycheque out of his back pocket and unfolded it. The white paper caught the sun. It shone. *Like one of those lucky wrappers in* Charlie and the Chocolate Factory, he thought. A winning ticket.

* * *

Charlotte stood at the wasp window, focusing on the stillness outside. At first it seemed completely intact, the stillness.

Then she began to notice cracks, slight undulations. The contrail of an airplane. Objects that eased across the blue —birds, boats, a few floaty clouds. Below the window a dragonfly hovered, then was gone. The waves of heat coming off the driveway made shapeshifters of ordinary things —the garden bench leaned back, the geraniums leaned forward, and Jacqueline's car was a hologram.

Rap, rap, rap. Charlotte turned toward the bedroom door, curious. She knew who it was. She'd heard the footsteps in the back of her mind, the light, steady footsteps. But the way the sound played into things, the sound of the footsteps and the sound of the knocking, the way they played into this illusion of stillness, was interesting.

Jacqueline carried the coffee on a small tray held in one hand. Her movements were delicate and fluid. She said nothing, set the tray down, stirred with a tiny spoon. Charlotte brought over an extra chair. When Jacqueline handed her the cup, they both smiled. It was the first time they'd seen each other since Saturday night.

They sat down. Jacqueline wasn't having coffee. She'd brought just the one cup. She picked a stray, black thread from her white blouse and placed it on the tray.

"I miss him already," she said. "Olivier." She folded her hands in her lap. "It always takes me by surprise, the missing. I never expect it. But he will be back soon enough."

Charlotte took a sip of her coffee and stopped smiling. The coffee was bitter, and she was used to drinking it with sugar. There was no sugar in this coffee. Charlotte frowned at the little spoon that Jacqueline had used to stir.

"He has a lot of faith in you," Jacqueline said. "He always has. And he tells me not to worry, that you will be fine. Theo too. He thinks you are fine."

Charlotte said nothing.

Jacqueline picked at her blouse again, but Charlotte couldn't see anything this time. Invisible thread.

"So, *ma chérie*," Jacqueline said. "How are you feeling?"

How am I feeling? Charlotte thought. She felt a little off balance. The spoon was confusing. The sugar, the no sugar. But that wasn't the question, was it? It was a bigger question, a question about her general state, not just this moment. How was she feeling? Excited. Yes, she did feel excited. Excited about how she saw things move. Like the things out the window. Things that at first didn't appear to move. Things that seemed to move beyond the confines of their mass.

Charlotte wondered about scientists, the ones who studied molecules and sound waves and a whole lot of stuff that she knew nothing about, and she had a picture of them in her mind, men in white lab coats going mad with hallucinations and voices in their heads, and she had the image of one lonely white-haired soul standing on a bluff in the Alps and letting out a big yodel just to see what would happen.

But that's as far as Charlotte got in the answer in her head because Jacqueline started talking again.

"Does your throat hurt? Is that the problem? It happens sometimes, you know. Or problems with the larynx. It is not uncommon for singers. We could see a specialist."

Charlotte shook her head.

Jacqueline sighed, then her eyes lit up. "Perhaps you could write it down. Here, let's find something." She went to Charlotte's desk. There was nothing on it but a lamp and a phone. Charlotte noticed the sparseness for the first time. *It's like a desk in a hotel room*, she thought, with nothing in the shallow drawer but a pad and a pen that she never used.

Jacqueline set the pad and pen in front of Charlotte then sat down across from her again and waited. Charlotte looked at the pad, the blank page. Blank, white page. The whiteness, it was stunning, and when she focused on it, it became like the stillness outside, not still at all. The blankness, not blank at all. It was full, fuller than it could ever be if she were to scribble all over it with words. It was full, complete, moving, evolving, perfect. And she didn't want to ruin it. *If I write on it*, she said to herself, *I will ruin it. If I speak, I will ruin it. I have nothing to say that is better than this*.

Charlotte looked at Jacqueline. She wanted her to see that it wasn't possible. She couldn't do it, couldn't write anything, couldn't say anything. Just couldn't do it.

Jacqueline's eyes darkened. Her fist flew up and slammed down on the table on top of the pad.

"Write!" she screamed. "Write something!"

The tray rattled with the coffee pot and the tiny spoon. And the pen, which had jumped a little, rolled slowly to the edge of the table and onto the floor.

Charlotte felt like she was going to cry. She desperately wanted Jacqueline to see, to understand, or even just to say that it was okay, that it was all okay. But Jacqueline had already looked away. She was standing now, smoothing the pleats of her skirt and the strands of her hair, though nothing was out of place.

"I cannot help you like this," she said in a low voice, and left.

That was it. She left the room, and the tray behind, and the door wide open, and a gap, a big gap. Charlotte cried.

After a couple of minutes, she stopped crying and put the empty cup on the tray. She saw the spoon there. And the black thread. And the invisible thread. And a drip of coffee where the spoon lay. She understood. She understood that she wasn't the way that Jacqueline needed her to be. Jacqueline needed her to be more normal, more normally functional. It was always the case. Not too normal, because then she wouldn't be special, but not too different either.

When anybody asked: *How are you feeling?* they didn't really want to know how she was feeling. They wanted to know whether she was going to be normal that day. They didn't want any surprises, anything too far out of the ordinary. Because if things were too far out of the ordinary, then they'd have to pay attention a little more, concentrate, and care. They didn't want to take the time. *But this is exactly what is required*, she thought. *I have to take the time. I have to look further. Reduce. Concentrate. Distil.*

* * *

It was downhill all the way home. Theo didn't stop, not once. And on a day with no breeze, it was glorious to feel the wind on his face. His new helmet was strapped to the handlebars, clacking against the aluminum as he raced. The avenues were wide and empty, and meandered their way down to the ocean. He could see for miles, across to the mountains and to Bowen Island, masses of dark green forest set against the blue of the sky and the blue of the water.

When he got to Jacqueline's driveway, he stopped. He wasn't sure whether to turn in or keep going. *There should be a lemonade stand*, he thought. That's exactly the kind of thing there should be at this moment. Kids selling lemonade outside their house. Maybe kids didn't do that anymore. Or maybe there just weren't any customers around here. Theo was the only one on the street.

He looked down the driveway. He thought about Charlotte in her room. Maybe he could ask her to come outside with him, go for a walk, get some fresh air. He remembered the tennis. Remembered her playing tennis with his dad. Outside. Sunny day. Not hot, but definitely sunny. Outside. Running. *What happens to people?* he wondered. Charlotte never went outside. At least when he was there. He'd never seen her go outside. Was it the sun? Was she staying out of the sun?

He left the house behind and took off again downhill. He thought about the past few weeks, rolling them through his mind, images of Charlotte, in the daytime, night-time, trying to capture a picture of her outside, on the terrace maybe, on a party evening, or drinking her tea in the afternoon. But he couldn't find her there. She was always just inside the door or by a window. He saw pictures of other people outside. He saw Curtis on the lawn, the girl named Margot and Olivier, as always, smoking. And the gazebo! He'd forgotten about that. He said he would build a gazebo in the backyard by the time Olivier got back. And Curtis said that Theo couldn't do it, that he never finished anything.

As Theo approached the beach, he had to slow down. It was only Monday, but the parking lots were full. Cars crawled along, waiting for spots to open up, but nobody was ready to leave. He rode right across the grass, watching the volleyballs and Frisbees and bikinis. He lifted the bike onto the sand. He was new to this bike thing and had no idea where to lock it up. He looked around. Nothing but logs and driftwood, and towels laid out in rows, children digging, couples reading magazines and talking on their phones.

He leaned the bike against a log. He took a picture of it and sent it to Curtis with the caption *Wheels*. Then he wondered if maybe he shouldn't have sent it. He still owed Curtis money. He wanted to swim, but the tide was way out, and he didn't feel like walking through all that squishy mud to get to the water. It wasn't the best swimming beach. Often, silt from the Fraser River churned up in the waves. He gave up on swimming and decided to ride down to the concession to buy a drink.

A gazebo might be just the thing for Charlotte.

TWENTY-FIVE

WHAT AN ODD *invitation*, Charlotte thought. Theo had knocked on her door and asked if she'd come down to dinner. Nothing more. Innocent enough. But the invitation felt formal, as though she was a guest in a guesthouse and Theo a messenger. She hesitated when he asked the question. She was still shaken by her conversation with Jacqueline earlier that day. But the truth was she wanted to go down. She wanted their company.

Jacqueline pulled the chair out for Charlotte. Theo sat across from her, tanned and radiant. Jacqueline took her place at the head of the table. It was only Olivier who was missing. Charlotte looked at his empty spot and caught a glimpse of herself in the oblong mirror that hung on the damask behind. She tilted her head to one side as if to align her face with the mirror, a portrait finding its frame. The bevelled edges of the mirror refracted light.

"It's a good sign that she has come down to join us," Jacqueline said to Theo.

Charlotte straightened up. They were talking about her as though she wasn't there.

"Maybe we can avoid a doctor after all," Jacqueline said. She looked to Charlotte now, and back to Theo. "Please, do begin."

Charlotte held her fork loosely in her hand. Theo was

watching her, and she wondered if there was already a plan to bring in a doctor. She didn't feel very hungry.

"Well, Charlotte," Theo said, raising his glass of wine, "you look healthy enough to me." They smiled at each other. She tried to eat a little.

Jacqueline wanted to know about Theo's audition the next day, so he told her about it, explaining that it wasn't for anything special, just a car commercial. Then she wanted to know if he'd ever thought about doing theatre. Yes, he'd thought about it but figured it wasn't really for him. Then he told them about the bike and how the people at the bike shop had all come over to take a look because it was vintage and in such good condition. Even the paint job, they said, was still good. Charlotte thought back to when she used to ride a bike. She was probably a teenager. And then Theo told them how he'd ridden down the hill without seeing a single car, and how the beach was packed, and how he'd come up with a great idea.

"I'm going to build a gazebo," he said.

Gazebo. *What a playful word*, Charlotte thought. She felt it buzz on her teeth as she said it silently in her head.

"It's for Charlotte," Theo said. "Well, and for Olivier. You see, I promised him. I promised him that by the time he got back, it would be done."

Jacqueline's eyes narrowed. She took a sip of wine between bites.

"Just think about it," Theo said. Charlotte loved the way Theo dropped his voice almost to a whisper, like they were all part of a conspiracy. "Olivier comes home, walks in the door, puts down his bags, wanders out to the terrace,

maybe to have a smoke, check out the night, and bam—
it's right there, in the middle of the backyard."

"The *backyard*?" Jacqueline asked, finally resting her
fork on her plate. "My garden, the backyard for your hut?"

"Well, it's not exactly a hut," Theo said.

"It sounds like a hut. And it sounds like after the hut
you will need a pit. For the bonfires. A nice pit. In the backyard. A hut. A pit. What else? Some tin cans for shooting?"

"No, no, it's not like that. Not tin cans. Get the tin cans
out of your head. Think old south, think southern hospi-
tality, serenades."

And he started to talk about the old south as if he'd
been there. He talked about Mississippi, Georgia, *Gone
with the Wind. It's like a ride*, Charlotte thought, the way
he talked. A river ride, swift, skipping from idea to idea,
and she was swept along. He talked about painting the
roof white. He used the word *filigree*, and that made Charlotte laugh. *Another playful word*, she thought, and coming out of Theo's mouth. He talked about Fred Astaire and
Ginger Rogers, and Charlotte tried to remember a song,
something about the rain.

Then Theo switched tracks and started to talk about
natural surroundings, maybe that was the way to go. Maybe
it was better to use natural tones and materials that would
blend in with the environment. Brown and green and grey.

"What about cedar?" he asked.

Then he talked about Charlotte, and the sun, and the
shade, and a bench with a cushion, and taking tea with
Olivier, and books, all the books that would be read inside
the gazebo.

Jacqueline's face remained unmoved, but she was sitting back in her chair now, listening.

"Like the Japanese ones!" Theo shouted.

"What Japanese ones?" Jacqueline asked.

"The ones in your books. With the pointy roofs. You know, the pagodas."

"You can build a pagoda?"

Theo stopped and thought about it seriously.

"No," he said after a while, "maybe not a pagoda. But a regular gazebo, sure. You'd like it, wouldn't you, Charlotte?"

Jacqueline was the only one not smiling. Charlotte wondered what Olivier would do if he was there. Surely he would smile too.

TWENTY-SIX

FOR THE AUDITION Theo was put in a group with two other guys and a girl, and the four of them had to show what a great time they were having driving their new four-wheel drive. They were going on a road trip up through the mountains and it was so fun that they couldn't stop laughing. What a blast. But the following day Theo got a message from his agent saying that he hadn't booked it. *Thank God for that*, Theo thought. But really, he was disappointed. He could've used the money. *Maybe it's my tan*, he thought. *I look too seasonal*.

He met a girl at the beach. Beatrice, from Quebec. Theo told her about Jacqueline being French, but Beatrice didn't seem to care. She asked Theo to take her to Wreck Beach so she could suntan nude. She didn't want to go by herself. *This is a strange way to get to know a girl*, he thought, watching her sit up and cross her legs and take the joint from him, naked.

The second day he saw her, he told her he was going to build a gazebo, and she shrugged. "If that's how you want to spend your summer," she said.

She didn't want him to kiss her when they were on the beach, or touch her in any way, but when they walked back up to the road at the end of each afternoon, she would take him off the path, and they'd pad their way over ferns until they were far enough out of sight, then she'd pull him to her with her back against a tree and they'd kiss and make love with their clothes mostly on.

After a few days, Theo stopped meeting up with her, stopped answering her texts. He was restless.

He got a message from Kenji saying that on Saturday they were all going down to the beach to play volleyball and he should come. Theo wondered if Curtis was going, but he didn't ask.

He didn't want to see Beatrice, but it was hard not to think about the sex in the woods. He thought about it more than anything. More than the gazebo. More than Curtis. And more than money. But he was going to run out of money before long, so he had to focus. He had to get more work. He called his agent. There was nothing right now. Summer was slow, his agent said.

Theo was having a cigarette on the terrace. Charlotte was upstairs. Jacqueline was out. He was staring at the big green lawn. The rest of the city had turned brown. Even the stretches of grass by the beach were dried up and yellow. But here the grass glowed green. Sometimes when Theo came home in the early hours of morning, instead of walking up the driveway, he'd walk across the lawn to cool his ankles in the automatic sprinklers.

He dialled Curtis' work number.

"Hey, I was expecting voice mail," Theo said when he heard the *hello*.

"Sorry," Curtis said. "You'll have to make do with the real me."

Theo asked him if he was going to the beach thing that Kenji was organizing.

"No, I don't think so," Curtis said.

"Why not?"

"I've got plans."

"What plans? It's the weekend."

There was a pause, and then Curtis said: "I've met someone."

"Really?" Theo was stunned. "You mean like a serious someone?"

"I hope so. His name is Matias."

"Where did you meet him?"

"The Running Room."

"What were you doing at the Running Room?"

"Buying runners."

"For what?"

"Running, asshole." Curtis hung up.

It took Theo a while to call back. First he had to have a cigarette. Then he had to go mix a drink because it was hot, and he was thirsty, and he was feeling sorry for himself. Then he had to have another cigarette because it went with the drink. And while he was having this second cigarette, he admitted to himself that he'd acted like a jerk. Curtis didn't swear much, so he must have been really pissed off.

Theo called back, expecting voice mail even more this time.

"What do you want?" Curtis said.

"To apologize. For being an asshole, just like you said. If you've started running, that's awesome. And if you've met someone, that's awesome too. I hope that it works out for you, man. I really do. And, well, the thing about the money. I'm going to get it to you as soon as I can. I've just got to get another gig."

Curtis didn't comment. He sighed and asked how Charlotte was doing.

Theo told him that she wasn't talking, and Curtis couldn't understand what the problem was.

"You mean you think she's choosing not to talk?" Curtis asked.

"Maybe."

"But that doesn't make any sense. What happened? Something must have happened. A trauma, or something."

"Nothing happened. At least not that I know of. She was talking on Saturday. Totally normal. Then she was supposed to sing. But she didn't actually sing. It was like … it seemed like she *thought* she was singing, but she wasn't. She was …"

"She was what? Humming? Mouthing the words? What?"

"No. I don't know, man. She wasn't doing anything."

"She needs to see someone."

"That's what Jacqueline says. But I don't know. It seems a bit extreme."

"You don't know what the problem is, Theo."

"You know, I hate the fact that whenever someone's not doing exactly what we want them to do, if they've strayed off a bit or they're having a bad day, we want to rush them to see someone. Get 'em fixed."

Curtis took a deep breath and let it out. "You're right," he said quietly. "You're right. But there could be a history."

"Yeah."

"Have you thought about asking your dad?"

Theo had thought about asking his dad but really didn't want to. His dad didn't even know he was living there.

"I don't know if he could handle it," Theo said. "He's too ... gone. He's so far gone. I don't get it. How do people change so much?"

"It's a bit of a mind-warp, isn't it?"

They agreed to get together soon. Theo could meet Matias.

After the call, Theo went inside and stood in the middle of the living room, looking at the stairs. He hadn't seen much of Charlotte lately. Or Jacqueline. It was two o'clock in the afternoon. He sent a text to Beatrice: *Beach?* He wondered why he hadn't mentioned her to Curtis. Usually he would mention something like that. He went out the front door and got on the bike.

TWENTY-SEVEN

Theo typed *how to build a gazebo* and found loads of photographs and videos showing muscle guys with hammers, and building plans where the diagrams didn't look like plans at all but delicate sketches. On one site there was a design for a square gazebo. *Square has to be easier than octagonal*, he thought. Still, the list of materials was daunting, and when he got to the part about pouring the footings and plumbing the posts, he put his phone back in his pocket.

***

Charlotte leaned forward in her chair and turned off the fan. It wasn't cooling her down, just blowing air into her face. She was relieved that no doctor had come to visit. Doctors never looked her in the eye. They glanced sideways or half-looked. She figured it was their way of being professional, keeping their distance. Or maybe they were just bored. Years ago she had gone to a therapist who acted like this —distant—and after a couple of sessions, the therapist wondered out loud whether the two of them were a good fit, as doctor and patient. Charlotte remembered shrugging her shoulders. What could she possibly say? She never booked another appointment.

It was after Johann and Theo had left. Sid kept insisting that she see someone. Charlotte didn't know what she'd expected, but it certainly wasn't that. Sid probably hoped she'd come back with a slew of prescriptions like the rest of them at the club. They were always popping something, washing it down with something else.

Charlotte stood up, her legs stiff from being in the same position for too long. She could hear Theo coming in from the terrace. She would go downstairs. They could play cards.

* * *

Theo had a new idea. This time he searched for gazebo kits that were ready to go. It turned out there were several local companies that sold pre-made kits, *affordable and easy to assemble*. But none of them looked easy to assemble, none of them had prices, and most of them were god-awful. There were gazebos with latticework, rock siding, glass windows, aluminum roofs, shingles, cupolas—that was a new word for Theo, *cupola*—built-in sinks and barbecues and hot tubs, gazebos that looked like mini log cabins, and cedar. Lots of cedar. He'd been right about that. One website featured a whole series of cedar structures that looked like parts of a Western theme park. *Add a few wagon wheels and some sawdust*, he thought, *and I can make myself a cowboy town. Hell, I may as well be sheriff.*

He went outside to look at the yard. He'd read that it was easier to build on level ground. The lawn was split in two by a path that led from the terrace to the back perimeter. The path wasn't straight down the middle. When you were standing on the terrace looking at the yard, it veered off to the left. So the biggest empty section was to the right. It was mostly flat but sloped down in the far right corner. Theo stood in the spot where he thought the gazebo would fit and ran his bare feet over the grass. It was soft.

He wondered if maybe it was too much trouble, the gazebo. It was a shame to cover the grass. Besides, there was a big umbrella on the terrace that provided enough shade for anyone who wanted it. He wondered if Beatrice would have sex in a gazebo. He wondered if she'd have sex in a bed.

* * *

Charlotte woke in a panic, imagining that Theo was in danger. She rushed into the hallway. The sun was starting to show, but the house was still asleep. Theo's door was closed. She didn't want to invade his privacy, but she *had* to open the door, check that he was okay. She turned the handle. It didn't make a sound. She pushed the door and looked in. She could see the shape of his body under the covers, and after a moment she heard his breathing. She closed the door, relieved. She started back to her own room but stopped part way and looked down the hall at Jacqueline's door. It was closed too.

* * *

Charlotte woke up again five hours later with an image of a door in her mind. Theo's door? No. It was Jacqueline's door. She got out of bed and put on her slippers, brilliant white in the sun that filled her room. Looking down the hallway, she saw that Jacqueline's door was open now and

Theo's still closed. The ceiling fan in the hall spun whispers. Charlotte listened. She looked out the hall window and saw the car in the driveway. Maybe Jacqueline was downstairs, or maybe in her room.

Charlotte walked slowly towards the open door. It occurred to her that she'd only been in Jacqueline's room a handful of times, just barely inside, and didn't really know what it looked like. The room had a magnificent view of the trees, and she'd always focused on that.

Charlotte approached cautiously, listening for the smallest sound of life inside.

"Are you afraid you'll find a body in there?" Charlotte gasped and turned around. It was Theo, standing in the doorway of his own room, grinning. "I'm sorry. I didn't mean to scare you."

She couldn't believe she hadn't heard him. Usually she heard everything. Even when she was concentrating on one thing, she would hear something else in the background. Maybe she'd been concentrating too hard. Maybe she'd managed to focus so intently on the sounds in Jacqueline's room that she was able to block out everything else.

She squeezed Theo tight. Relieved. She just felt so relieved.

"Come and look," he said, leading her to the window in his own room that looked over the backyard. "There she is."

Jacqueline was standing on the edge of the terrace, facing the garden.

"What do think?" Theo asked, his arm around Charlotte's shoulder. "Do you think she's visualizing the amazing gazebo I'm going to build? Somehow I doubt it."

As Charlotte relaxed, she became conscious of sounds. She heard some birds. Not the early songbirds but the crows and starlings. She heard a lawn mower a couple of doors down and some banging, hammering. Traffic in the distance. And a clicking, close by, probably in the garden below, an insect, the clicking of wings.

* * *

Theo had another idea. This time he looked up the big hardware stores, the home renovation stores, and found that they had kits too and would even do the installation. But that was kind of cheating, and besides, what they offered was worse than the cedar cowboy shacks. Tents basically. Then Theo thought about the library. Maybe he could find a how-to book there, a *Gazebos for Dummies*. He wondered where the library was.

* * *

Walls of sky. That's what Charlotte remembered most about that evening years ago. The walls of black sky and shaking Jacqueline's hand.

It was about a year after Johann had left. Sid was done with her. She'd downsized to a tiny apartment and was booking weddings and parties to pay the rent. Lots of rich people dressed up and drinking. This party was no different except the windows in that condo were two storeys high. There was so much glass and so much black.

The handshake was unexpected. Not the introduction itself, but the nature of the handshake, the warmth of it, the way Jacqueline wrapped Charlotte's outstretched hand in both of hers and just held it. It was the first time they'd met. Jacqueline asked Charlotte if she'd like to perform at another party a week from then. She said yes.

From there, she pretty much moved right in. Just like Theo. One morning she woke up in a new room and stayed. Before long she had a closet full of gowns and shoes. She was happy to give up the tiny apartment she could barely afford, happy to leave behind her old life. It was liberating, exhilarating. And it felt safe. That was the thing. She felt safe with Jacqueline.

Charlotte looked at the sealed wasp window behind its chintz curtains. She had laughed at all the chintz when she had first arrived. Then she got used to it.

* * *

Theo came across a design he really liked. It was another square gazebo, built in the woods near the ocean, or maybe a lake—it was hard to tell from the picture. He liked the feel of it. It looked like a good place to take a nap. He would definitely need a saw. There might be one in the garage. A saw and a hammer he could handle, but beyond that, he wasn't so sure. He wondered if his buddy O'Brian would help him out. O'Brian was in construction. But he might have moved to Calgary. Theo couldn't remember.

"Why are you doing this?" Beatrice asked him on the beach that afternoon when he was searching again on his phone. She wasn't very impressed by the gazebo he'd shown her, the one by the water. "What are you trying to prove?"

She had a hat over her face and a big scarf wrapped around her torso because she didn't want to burn in the two o'clock sun. She lay perfectly still, like an exotic food wrapped in a banana leaf.

"I'm not trying to prove anything," he answered. But he had to wonder.

* * *

Charlotte sat at the desk in her room—the hotel desk, as she thought of it now. *How did I get here?* She was trying to retrace her steps, map out the years, but the years didn't line up with starts and ends and milestones but blended, blurred, piled themselves one on top of the other in a mass of time, outlines faded, definition lost. *How did I get here?* Desk furnished by Jacqueline. Desk, chair, bed, chintz. Everything furnished by Jacqueline. The heat pressed. Perspiration beaded on Charlotte's breastbone. The empty pad of paper was on the desk, one edge curled.

Don't make me talk, she addressed the blank paper. *Don't make me muddy things with words. With casings. Shells. Beginnings and endings and once upon a time, the story. We don't always need a story. Don't make me tell a story. There's nothing to tell. Don't do it. Don't set me up. Don't put me on the bill and expect the same thing again and again. Don't set me up. Don't expect me. Don't expect me to play it again and again and again and again, Sam. Don't.*

So many *don'ts*. Charlotte couldn't stop the words. Even though her mouth was shut, the words flowed in her thoughts. Thoughts manifested in language. She couldn't erase the language. To do that she would have to erase the thoughts, and she didn't want to erase the thoughts. *Don't. Don't. Don't.*

TWENTY-EIGHT

THEO FOUND THE library. By accident. He was getting a coffee and the library happened to be a couple of doors down from the café, right where he'd locked up the bike. He went in and found the section with books about homes and gardens and Do It Yourself. He looked through several of them and picked three that had gazebos. They were large, hardcover books, and he wasn't sure he'd be able to fit them in the rat trap on the bike. If he had to, he could carry them under one arm and steer with the other.

But when he went to the desk with the big sign that said Library Cards, there was a problem. To get a card he needed identification and proof of residence, and he'd left all that back at the house.

"A wallet's too heavy to carry around everywhere," he explained to the librarian. "Especially in summer."

She didn't look like she cared about summer. She was wearing a sweater. And her face was greyish. She didn't look pleased either. *Maybe*, Theo thought, *she's pissed off because she has to work all day and can't go to the beach. No, she doesn't like the beach. She hates the beach. And she hates me because I made her get up out of her chair. And I don't even have the proper ID.*

The librarian had nothing to suggest. She just turned

her back. Theo slammed the three books down on the counter, ready to storm out. This caught her attention, and when her grey skin turned red, Theo changed his mind about leaving.

"All right then!" He swept the books back into his arms. Several people were staring. "I'll just have to read them here."

His adrenalin was still pumping while he flipped through the pages of *Backyard Structures — Everything You Need to Know*, full of a bunch of stuff that he really didn't care to know. *It's got to be easier than this*, he thought, pushing the book aside.

Build the Backyard of Your Dreams was a joke. The gazebos looked like oversized dollhouses. In one photo a little boy stood outside the gazebo, his elbow resting on the railing like he'd sidled up to a bar, while his mother, standing inside, poured him a glass of lemonade from a big jug. Two other kids sat in the shade playing a board game, a spaniel at their feet with its tongue hanging out. It was hard to tell whether the dog was panting or yawning or licking its lips. *Definitely out of the question*, he thought. Jacqueline hated kids.

The third book didn't talk about how to *build* structures but how to *imagine* them, how to incorporate them into a garden. The glossy pages showed rustic gates, painted doorways, fences, walls, trellises, the pergolas that Theo had read about online, meandering paths, patios, decks, greenhouses. Theo took a picture of an arbour with a bench that looked simple enough. But the page he was really drawn to showed a swimming pool and a patio with a long rustic table under the vines. *Another world*. He snapped a few more pictures, soliciting a dirty look from a lady sitting across the table.

***

Charlotte was holding Theo's phone, looking at the photograph he'd taken especially for her—a garden, a clearing with bricks laid in concentric circles.

"It's from a book," he said. "I didn't actually go there. Obviously."

But it wasn't obvious. There was an intimacy to the picture, and a realness. What first struck Charlotte was the stream of sunlight that hit just off centre. Late afternoon light that cut through the trees. There was a large round stone with water running onto it from a tap. Around the bricks were shrubs and saplings, purple flowers and tall grasses, not arranged in any particular order, but not in disorder either, as though all the plants had stepped up to see what was going on, to hear the news. Everything stood where it stood, focused on the middle. The empty middle.

***

Theo was considering the lawn again, having a hard time reconciling it with the Mediterranean gardens he'd seen in that third book at the library, and wondering if maybe Olivier was in one of those gardens now in the South of France. He sat at the top of the slope, looking at the forest behind, the cedars tall, silent sentinels. He did a summersault down the little hill. It felt good. He did another, and another, and ended up with his feet in the dirt. It was dry, all the moisture from the sprinkler long evaporated. His phone rang. It was his agent. Another audition. *Thank God*, he thought. Maybe he could keep the restaurant jobs at bay for another day.

A crow cawed loudly from the trees then flew directly over his head and up to the roof of the house where other crows were congregating. *What are they up to?* He turned and watched Joy come outside waving a broom.

"Go away, go away," she called, but she didn't sound very threatening, and the crows didn't go away. She noticed Theo sitting way down at the back of the yard.

"It's the plums," she shouted. "They get the plums from trees on the street and bring them here. Messy, messy," she said taking her broom to the terrace.

So that's what they were doing—eating plums and dropping pits. It reminded Theo of the crows he saw at the beach dropping mussels onto the pavement from high in the air to smash the shells so they could eat the insides. Sometimes it took several tries before the shell would break. He loved watching the crows. They were crafty. They perched on garbage cans, sipped from water fountains, stood on logs, watching sandwiches being unwrapped, waiting for their moment. Once Theo saw a crow unwrap a sandwich and fly off with half of it, bits of tomato falling out, as a sopping wet man back from his swim yelled and flapped his arms.

Theo had seen crows descend discreetly on empty baby strollers to peck out Cheerios from plastic cups. And when a baby was left alone, Theo worried the crows might descend on it too. But they never did. They just watched and waited. The seagulls were bolder. They didn't wait in the wings like the crows but walked straight up to whoever had the fries, whoever had the ice cream. They were beggars and raiders, while the crows were thieves, creative and resourceful.

***

"Here, you should take this." Theo held out a pill bottle to Charlotte, and she felt panicky for a split second until she read the label. *Vitamin D.* "For the sun. Because you don't go outside."

When she didn't take it, he put it back in the cupboard with the rest of Jacqueline's collection. *Vitamin D, Vitamin E* ... Charlotte could hear Theo as a boy reading the ingredients listed on the bottle of Flintstones at the kitchen table. She could see him digging for Barney.

"There's something else," he said. "About the gazebo." He hesitated. He didn't usually hesitate, and Charlotte smiled to reassure him. "When it's all done, when it's finished—if I ever get that far—if you don't want to go in it ... it's okay, I won't mind."

***

Theo sat on a log and smoked the rest of the joint. Beatrice had gone to work. She worked in a restaurant downtown. There was a party crowd a way along the beach, Mexicans and Quebecois. Maybe he'd wander down. There was a fort in front of him, no doubt built by kids. It was made from logs and driftwood and busted up boards from a home-made skateboard ramp, covered in graffiti. It was a pretty good fort. Too small for Theo to sit inside, but big enough for little kids, he imagined. The section right in front of him was built like a tipi, with a circle of logs and sticks standing on end and meeting in the middle. There was a flag at the top made of seaweed that had probably been fished out of the water wet but was now dry and brittle. Theo heard a rustle in the brambles off to the side. He looked closely and saw a rabbit. Then another. And another. There must have been at least fifteen rabbits just in that little patch. He wondered if the rabbits ever went into the fort, when nobody was there.

The tipi had a way in, a front door. And on the opposite side, a tunnel. *There must be a back door too*, he thought, *so you can access the tunnel from the tipi*. The tunnel was quite high. The kids could probably walk through it if they crouched a little. *How did they get it to stand up like that?* He got up off the log and went to look. Thick sticks and plywood from the skateboard ramps had been used to make the walls. They had been jammed into the sand. *Or maybe the sand was dug out by shovels*, Theo thought, noticing a plastic shovel lying a few feet to the side, cracked and faded yellow. The base of the walls had been stabilized with piles of sand.

Theo imagined an army of kids reinforcing the walls, the littlest ones being sent to fetch buckets of water to make the dry sand wet. Theo pressed one of the sticks. It moved a bit. It wasn't solid in the ground. He pressed another. And a piece of plywood. They all had a bit of give. But the pieces that made up the roof were keeping it all together. A balancing act. Theo went around the opening of the tunnel and looked through to the tipi. Sure enough, there was a back door.

* * *

The moon was blank too, like the notepad on the hotel desk, like the middle of the clearing, blank and expecting. Charlotte couldn't fight it. The thoughts came whether she conjured them or not. Maybe it was best just to let them in, let them pass through. Thoughts about Theo, how he didn't pressure her to speak—she was grateful for that —and how he'd made a specific point of excusing her from the outdoors, and the vitamins—it used to be her making sure that he was eating enough vegetables. And she remembered the time Johann came home from work to find the two of them sitting on the front porch, Theo grinning sticky Popsicle juice, and she with her legs stretched out in the summer evening—Johann shot her such a look of disapproval that she felt ashamed of her bare toes and the wrappers and wooden Popsicle sticks strewn on the steps. Later, when Theo was in bed, Johann joked over wine that she wasn't really cut out for motherhood, was she? It was the first time she thought of Johann as unkind.

She didn't want to remember these things. Not now. They were in the way. Filters. Obstructing the light. Clouds drifting over the face of the moon. She reached out to brush them away, but her hand swiped at darkness. The distance mocked her, and the thoughts kept rolling in—Johann's cruelty, his derision, his briefcase, the coffee she used to drink when everyone had left in the morning, the tomato plants in the neighbour's backyard, the streets of Chinatown, the small boy who needed someone to walk with him through the neighbourhood, the walking together—it had been one of her favourite things. Charlotte draped her arms over the sill and felt the wooden siding of the house, rough and dusty. *Sorry.*

The thought came from her like a whisper. And stayed. It didn't drift on, didn't pass through. *Sorry.* She was sorry about the sun, sorry that she couldn't go outside, just couldn't, and couldn't organize herself in a way like other people organized themselves. Why couldn't she organize herself? Do the things she needed to do, she'd done before? Why not now? *Sorry.* She was sorry she couldn't find the words, the out-loud words. For Theo.

She snatched her hands back inside. A splinter stuck out from under her fingernail.

* * *

Jacqueline was banging on his door, telling him to get up now and get downstairs.

"Okay, okay," Theo yelled at the door. "I'll be down in a second."

What the hell was going on? Water. He needed water. It was painful to stand up. Standing up made his head hurt more. *What could possibly be going on?*

Jacqueline was waiting at the bottom of the stairs, and there was something about the whole scene that Theo couldn't stand. He half expected her to tweak his ear as he walked by and out the front door in the direction she was pointing.

There on the driveway, at the foot of the steps, was a giant heap of driftwood.

Theo started to laugh. "Holy shit!" he said. "Holy fucking shit! That's a lot of wood."

Jacqueline glared.

"I completely forgot," he said, putting his hands in the air, trying to stop laughing. "When you woke me up, I had absolutely no recollection. And now that I see it, I remember everything. Shane! This guy Shane drove me. We threw it all in the back of his pickup. I had the whole beach helping me."

Jacqueline didn't say a thing. She was breathing slowly and deliberately, staring straight at Theo. *This is it*, he thought. *She's definitely going to kick me out.*

After a few moments, she looked away, almost absently, like she was looking at the sky for an indication of what the weather would bring. Clear sky. Hot sun. She unzipped her purse and drew out her car keys. They jangled.

She looked back at Theo, but all the heat in her expression was gone now.

"Move it," she said, indicating the pile of wood with a nod.

Theo watched her get into the car. He knew exactly what it was that he couldn't stand. Being pushed around. The car edged past the wood and drove away. Theo looked up to Charlotte's window. It was in the shadows. He sat down on the top step.

Well, she didn't say get rid of the wood. She just said move it.

TWENTY-NINE

THE TRUCK HAD come in the night, rumbling up the driveway. The engine was cut, the radio too, and the voices hushed themselves. The doors of the truck opened, closed. Charlotte got out of bed and went to the wasp window, still afraid to open it. She peered down into the pool of light, cast by the porch lamps, where moths danced. It was Theo. And another man, tall, slim, with long, black hair, older than Theo. The back of the truck was stacked high with a jumble of driftwood. The man opened the tailgate. It creaked, and the wood shifted. He climbed into the bed of the truck and started handing pieces to Theo, who tossed them onto the pavement.

They worked like this for a few of minutes, a chain of two, the rhythm punctuated by hollow steps in the bed of the truck and clacks made when the wood hit the pile. And then they were down to the last bits, and the rhythm broke, and the man hauled a big log to the edge, scraping it on the steel. Theo took the end and dragged the log onto the heap. The man jumped down, slammed the tailgate shut, and shook hands with Theo. They laughed, said a few words that Charlotte couldn't hear, and then there was the door and the engine and the radio again, and the truck coasted back down the driveway, lighter and quieter now. Theo stared at the pile of wood then went inside.

Now, several hours later, in the light of day, Charlotte watched Theo stand in the exact same spot and stare at the wood again. She wondered what he was going to do with it. She wondered if he knew about the wheelbarrow behind the garage. She felt her hand reach slightly in that direction —an impulse, a wish—and she felt the resistance. She was caught. She knew it. Trapped. Cornered. She'd cornered herself. The pad of paper was still there on the desk, blank and bright in the white sunlight that washed over the room. And she remembered a time when she was a child. A boy in the neighbourhood—she couldn't remember his name—showed her how to light a fire using a magnifying glass and the rays of the sun.

He wanted to burn things. A newspaper, her front lawn, a stick, beetles on the sidewalk. But she didn't want to burn the beetles, so she went into the house to find something else, something she could sacrifice to save the beetles. She saw her paper dolls laid out on the desk in her room. There were three of them. She dressed each one in their favourite outfit and laid them carefully one on top of the other with the tabs tucked tightly so that the paper clothes wouldn't fall off. She carried them outside, her palms keeping them in place, but stopped before she reached the sidewalk.

Fire. There was real fire. The boy had piled up some dry grass and leaves and covered them with sticks and made a miniature bonfire. It was small, but it burned strong. And she could see the danger. It was close to the lawn, and on the lawn there were bushes, and the bushes led to the house. *What do you have?* the boy called out. She came closer and opened her hands, showing him the paper dolls.

Throw them on, he said. She didn't want to. She didn't want to burn them anymore. She didn't want to sacrifice them. She wanted to turn back but she was embarrassed.

She wondered what had happened to the beetles. She saw one by her feet. Maybe they'd escaped. *Throw them on,* the boy said again. And she did. The paper dolls caught fire instantly, the edges curling, the colours intensifying briefly, turning shiny, then black. A hat had fallen off to the side. One of the doll's hats. A straw hat. She looked at it lying on the sidewalk, figuring out how to pick it up without getting too close to the fire, but the boy snatched it up and threw it on, and at the same time her mother rushed out screeching and grabbed the garden hose.

Then the fire was out, and there was a puddle of black and brown debris. The boy ran away with his magnifying glass. And Charlotte started to cry. Her mother yelled and pulled her up the front path, along with the hose. A cold trickle of water from the hose ran down her neck and arms and made her cry even more.

When Charlotte looked out the window again, Theo was gone. She didn't like the way Jacqueline had talked to him. It was mean. She'd never thought of Jacqueline as mean.

***

When Theo got out of bed again, Charlotte made coffee, and they drank it in the living room, the terrace doors open. He was talking about his dad and kept tapping his fingers on his cup.

"I don't talk to him much these days," he said. "I've

barely seen him since moving back to Vancouver. He didn't want me to come out here. Said I could just as well be an actor in Toronto. But he doesn't even like the acting. Says it's not a real job." Theo looked out to the terrace. "I haven't told him about you. That you're here. That I'm here. I'm sure he thinks I still live with Curtis. I kind of want to tell him, but I'm afraid he'll wreck it, which is crazy because I don't know how he could possibly wreck anything, what he could actually do, but I think he'd try to make me leave or something. The thought of it ... him just showing up at the door ... it's my worst nightmare."

Charlotte had thought about this too, Johann knocking at the front door, and Jacqueline opening it. *May I help you?*

"Imagine the four of us sitting around the dinner table," Theo said. "You, me, Jacqueline, my dad. You know, just catching up, drinking some wine." Theo started to laugh. "That's some good comedy." He stretched his arms behind his head and looked out to the terrace again. "What is with this weather? It won't stop. It's like we live in paradise all of a sudden." He picked up his coffee cup and drank what was left then carefully placed the cup back on the coaster, turning the handle slightly and straightening the coaster so it was aligned with the sides of the table. Charlotte noticed the precision. It was unusual for Theo.

"He wasn't always like that, was he?" Theo said. "Do you think he figured he had to be doubly responsible, since he was the only parent? Maybe it just caught up with him, all the responsibility. You know what I mean?"

Charlotte knew exactly what he meant. She'd watched it happen. At first Johann was all adventure and spontaneity.

Picnics in the living room, gelato on summer nights way past Theo's bedtime, stopping to listen to music in the streets. He said he liked that Charlotte wasn't a regular girl who just wanted a diamond ring and liked that she could make friends with just about anyone. But then he started to worry about things. And push. He said Charlotte should quit the club and find an accompanist to work with. Or teach. She could teach.

He started complaining about the neighbourhood, said it wasn't good for Theo. He wanted to buy a house, in a better part of town. He wanted more nine to five. He wanted the family to sit down to dinner together. And a wife who was around on a Friday night. He wanted Theo to play baseball in the spring and hockey in the winter. And he didn't want her, didn't want Charlotte. Not after a while.

Charlotte breathed deeply into a little corner of her self. She had nowhere to go but further in. Theo was sitting forward on the edge of the couch, looking outside. *He needs to get out*, she thought. She'd cornered herself, but she didn't want to corner Theo. She didn't want him to stay just for her. He needed to get out, to leave. He didn't need to sit by her and watch. She didn't want him to. She wanted him to move, to run. He should run.

He looked over at her for a moment then stood up and went outside. She watched him light a cigarette, wander onto the lawn, drag his feet along the grass. Every once in a while, he'd lift his head up to the sky as if he was sensing something on the air, a breeze, a scent. *There's a lot more to him than people realize*, she thought.

THIRTY

THEO WAS STARING at the trees with a pair of miniature binoculars searching for the woodpecker. Wearing nothing but a pair of shorts, he looked like an under-aged birder who'd spent too much time in the woods.

"Where are you, you little fucker?" he said under his breath.

He caught sight of something in his peripheral vision. It was Jacqueline, coming outside. She sat down in a chair near to where he was standing. He wondered what she'd say about the wood. He'd piled it right onto the back lawn.

"Nice little gift, those," Jacqueline said, putting her feet up.

"What's that?"

"The opera glasses. Your friend gave them to me. The little friend of Grigore."

Theo lowered the glasses and turned them over in his hand. "These are opera glasses?"

"1960s," Jacqueline said. "In fact, they're remarkably similar to my very first pair."

She reached out her hand and Theo passed the glasses. She raised them and stared over at the neighbours' house, then brought them level and stared at Theo.

"Don't look so surprised," she said. "I too can watch

the world go by." She examined them, turning them over in her hand as Theo had done. "I wonder where he found them."

Theo remembered the package now, the little wrapped box. It was just the kind of thing Curtis would come up with.

"There's no improvement," Jacqueline said. "Is there?"

"Are you talking about Charlotte? She's still not speaking, if that's what you mean." He sat down and picked up his cigarettes from the table.

"Well, I've invited some people for Saturday. I wanted to wait until Olivier was back, but I have a friend in town I'd like to you to meet. Besides, I'm bored."

Theo kept quiet, lit his cigarette.

"You will help me, won't you, Theo?"

He glanced at her. Where was this going?

"Finn Lockie, the filmmaker, he's a friend of mine." Jacqueline said. "Do you know him?"

"No."

"He is shooting a short film here, in Tofino actually. And he needs a boy. I told him you would be perfect. I'll arrange it. Before the party though. Get business out of the way."

Sure, go right ahead. Sign me up. Don't bother asking or anything. Theo took a long pull on his cigarette.

"There's no money," Jacqueline said. "You would do it because you wanted to. And believe me, with Lockie, you want to."

You don't know what I want.

"And another thing," Jacqueline said. "On Saturday, Charlotte will sing."

"Really. How's that going to happen?"

Jacqueline stretched out her arms, clasped her hands behind her head, turned her face to the sun and closed her eyes.

"I don't know how it's going to happen," she said, her eyes still shut. "That's where you come in. I know I can count on you."

What game is this? Theo thought. *What insane game is this?* He picked up his glass. It was empty. He wanted to chuck it across the yard, hurl it at the fence. He wanted out. Out of this place, this house, this yard. He hated this yard, with the path, and the flowers that lined the path, and the fence, and everything always trimmed, and the grass that was so, so green when the rest of the city was brown, and he hated how much he loved to trail his bare feet across this beautiful, green grass.

His pile of driftwood was pathetic. He'd thought it was so fucking hilarious dumping it on the back lawn. Now he just wanted it gone.

"I'm parched," Jacqueline said. She stood up. "Shall I fetch us a drink?" She took Theo's empty glass from his hand.

"That's right!" he said. "Feed Theo another drink. Then he'll do whatever you want!"

He grabbed his phone and cigarettes and took off around the side of the house, heading for the bike, propped up against the garage. Goddamn it. He didn't have any shoes on.

THIRTY-ONE

THEO DECIDED NOT to hide it. When he came home that evening, he sat on the white couch across from Charlotte and told her about Saturday. "You're supposed to sing," he said.

How? For a moment Charlotte wondered if she had spoken the word out loud, but she hadn't.

"And I'm supposed to make it happen," Theo said. "She's nuts. You know that she's nuts." He glanced around. "She's not here, is she?"

Charlotte shook her head slowly, processing the information.

"I'm hungry." Theo got up to go to the kitchen. "Do you want anything?" Again she shook her head.

As soon as Theo had left the room, Charlotte stood up and walked toward the open doors, her hands shaking, her face growing hot. Jacqueline didn't have the dignity to deliver her own message. Instead she'd used Theo. And more than that, she'd charged Theo with getting Charlotte to sing, knowing that Charlotte would do anything she could for Theo. It was cheap. Calculated. Jacqueline was using them. Manipulating them. Because that's what she did.

Charlotte watched the fan blow the gauzy curtains outside, inside, outside. Her forehead was coated with sweat, and her stomach was seized up like a fist. She'd shut it out, hadn't she? She'd shut it out all these years because she'd wanted to believe that she was different, that she was special to Jacqueline in a way that nobody else was.

Theo brought in a sandwich on a plate and a glass of milk. He ate half the sandwich in a few bites and put the plate on the coffee table. He took a swig of milk. Charlotte was watching the curtains move.

"Have you ever thought of leaving?" he asked.

Charlotte didn't know the answer to this. She'd never had the conscious idea of leaving, never thought *I want to go*, but now she had a feeling of wanting to leave—an inclination.

"It's possible," Theo said, picking up the other half of his sandwich. "You should think about it."

* * *

Theo spent a lot of time away from the house, leaving around noon and coming home in the evening, restless, hungry. He had things on his mind. Sometimes he'd share them with Charlotte. Eventually he'd wind up outside staring at the pile of wood and poking at it with his feet before taking off to meet someone somewhere, usually the beach. Beatrice wasn't around much these days. Theo didn't want to admit it, but he missed her. He missed Curtis too.

Sometimes he talked to Charlotte about Curtis, or acting, or what he'd done that day. Sometimes he brought up the subject of his father, not knowing where to take it, but curious. Sometimes he talked about when he was a kid.

"Remember the lady who used to sing on the bus?" he asked.

Charlotte remembered. It was the bus she took to the club. And the one she and Theo took to the pool for his swimming lessons on Saturdays. The lady used to get on the bus at the tent park, loaded up with plastic bags. She'd push her way down the aisle to the back, and occasionally, if they were lucky, she'd break out in song. Full voice. Opera. Theo's face would light up every time. Usually she'd wait until she got off the bus before starting to sing. The regulars would wait too, smiling discreetly. They'd watch her descend the stairs, wrestling with her bags and the automatic doors. They'd wait for the moment her foot hit the pavement and the song began. There'd always be someone on the sidewalk who'd jump back in surprise, and the regulars on the bus would chuckle to themselves. Charlotte thought she was marvellous.

"Remember that time with the tickets?" Theo asked. "The time when she handed a ticket to the bus driver, and he refused it. So she reached into her pocket and brought out another one. And he refused that one too. Then she found another and another, and it kept on going, and she kept on reaching into different pockets and bags and bringing out pieces of paper that weren't even bus tickets anymore, and then finally the bus driver just said forget it and waved her on."

Charlotte remembered. It was priceless.

"She gave me a quarter once," Theo said. "She said it was her way of paying taxes. I asked her what taxes were, and she said it was the thing you had to do in order to convince people you weren't crazy. *That*, and *recycling*, she said. She said that as long as you could separate glass from tin, people would leave you alone."

* * *

On another occasion, Charlotte and Theo were making coffee together in the kitchen.

"It must be hard to listen so much," he said. "To just listen and watch."

There was new understanding between them.

* * *

Charlotte felt restless too. She went to the wasp window where Theo had been standing earlier that day and looked up to the eaves as he had done. She couldn't see anything there. She touched her fingers to the glass. Her skin crawled. She tried to shake it off, a feeling of separation, skin from self. She panicked, rushed to the mirror, but it was all there, all her skin. She'd had a flash, a memory of Mae, West End Mae, sitting in the dressing room, peeling off patches of skin from her forehead, red flaky skin. Charlotte caught her eye in the mirror. *I can't make it stop*, Mae said. *No matter what I do, it won't go away.* She dabbed her face with a cotton pad. *Thank God for make-up*, she said.

Charlotte touched her own face. Her skin was perfectly smooth. *Sorry.* The word pushed from inside again but didn't come out. Charlotte draped a scarf over the mirror so she couldn't see herself anymore.

THIRTY-TWO

CURTIS DIDN'T KNOW what to suggest. "You can't take care of her. You can barely take care of yourself."

"I know, I know, it's true," Theo said.

"And maybe that's not what she needs anyway."

"Maybe."

The place looked different. The kitchen had been repainted, the living room too. Posters had been taken down. The broken TV was gone. And Taylor had moved out after only two weeks. Apparently she'd met some guy and moved in with him right away.

"It was a bad idea from the start," Curtis said. "But she paid a month's rent."

He told Theo that Matias was probably going to move in. They were thinking of turning Theo's bedroom into a den and making the living room more of a dining area.

"Sounds domestic," Theo said.

"Insanely domestic," Curtis said, grinning. "I've got to get you guys together one of these days."

Theo closed his old front door behind him, the question of Charlotte still unanswered. He felt like he was running out of time.

* * *

Beatrice didn't want to see Theo anymore. At first she'd just stopped answering his texts, then she sent a message saying she was going to Whistler for a while. Theo didn't really care. She wasn't a real girlfriend anyway.

***

Curtis called. "I've got an address for you," he said. "Charlotte's old friend, Sid. I had a lead."

"Why would I want to talk to this guy?"

"Because he might be able to give you some advice."

"I don't need advice. I need a fucking time machine."

"To go back to *when*?" Curtis asked.

"Not back. Forward!"

***

Theo was starting to feel that the phone call was a mistake. The more his dad talked, the more irritable he became. When was Theo coming out? He should come during the summer so they could go to the cottage. Could he take time off work? What about a ticket? They could help him out. Had he looked at prices recently?

Theo took a deep breath. He didn't want to back out. He'd called for a specific reason—to talk about Charlotte. He wanted to understand what was going on. He wanted to help her. And he wanted to know the truth.

"I've found Charlotte," Theo said, cutting his father off.

The pause was a lot longer than Theo expected. Finally his dad asked what he meant by *found*.

"It's not important how it happened, but, well, I live with her."

"Live with her?" his dad asked. Theo realized how it sounded and explained that they weren't *living together* but that they lived in the same house.

"What house?" The voice was getting louder now, aggressive, and Theo felt a pinching in his chest. He looked out the window, breathed deeply. He wanted to hang up, but he wanted to know.

"We left her, didn't we?" Theo asked. Again there was a long pause. "We left Charlotte, didn't we?"

"We had to."

"But you told me she wanted us to go."

"It wasn't clear-cut."

"No? Then explain it to me."

Theo expected almost anything—tales of madness, mental illness, drama, violence, drugs. Maybe his dad tried to help Charlotte, tried to make her better. Maybe he fought to keep them all together. Some kind of struggle.

"We weren't aligned," his dad said. "She had no ambition. No desire to increase her income, make a proper career. And she started doing weird music."

That was it? He wanted her to make more money? And he didn't like the music? Theo was struck by the coldness of it. *Why am I sticking around for this? Hang up. Hang up the phone.*

"One last thing," Theo said. "Did you ever know a guy named Sid?"

"You mean that fairy who ran the club?"

"That would be the one."

THIRTY-THREE

THEO WAS GRINDING his way up the hill, crouched forward over the handlebars. The highest part of the day was gone, but the heat dragged. He'd smoked a lot of weed at the beach and hadn't eaten for a while. He felt sick. He pushed down onto the pedals, forcing them to crank forward, right then left, his head down. He gasped suddenly and fell off the bike onto the curb, coughing. He'd ridden straight into a cloud of midges and sucked one into lungs. He wheezed, trying to get it out. An SUV roared past, pulsating with bad music. He sat in its wake and looked around. *What is this place? What is this empty place?*

He was thirsty. He was always thirsty. He wondered how he would ever survive in the wilderness, or after a disaster or an earthquake. How would he find water? Food? He should figure that out. He should learn what to do, just in case. But for now, all he had to do was stand up and walk another two blocks and turn on a tap.

Two days to Saturday, and he didn't have a plan.

He walked the bike back to the house and leaned it against the garage. He went in through the back terrace. He didn't want to run into Jacqueline. He listened for her but heard nothing. In the kitchen he turned on the tap and let the water stream into his mouth. He could taste the salt from his skin. He poured himself a glass of orange juice, and another, and stared into the fridge.

He thought about going upstairs to see Charlotte, but his feet were black with dirt, and Charlotte's room was full of white and stillness, and he was irritable and restless and stoned and needed to be outside.

He stood on the pile of wood, teetering on a plank. He couldn't let go of the conversation he'd had with his dad, couldn't get it out of his system. *What did I expect?* He jumped a couple times on the spot, testing the bend in the board. He'd hoped that his dad might have given him some insight, some ideas, or at least might have been interested in what Theo had to say, but it didn't work out that way, and they never got to the heart of the matter. They barely got past hello.

Theo picked up a long piece of wood, held it firmly with two hands and jammed it into the ground. It stuck for a second, leaned, then fell over onto the pile with a clatter. His dad really didn't care about people. He only cared about himself. A mosquito passed in front of Theo's face. Another landed on his arm. He swatted it. The sun was going down. He needed a shower, but he didn't want a shower. He went inside to the kitchen and sprayed himself with mosquito repellent, all over his skin and clothes, rubbing some onto his face.

When he went back outside, he'd made up his mind. It was time to build. Something. Anything. He just couldn't stand looking at that pile of wood anymore.

He went to the garage and gathered a few things—a trowel, a hammer, some pieces of rope of varying thicknesses and a spool of wire. On his way out he saw a pair of flowery gardening gloves on the edge of the workbench and grabbed those too.

The gloves were stiff and a ladies' size small, but he

squeezed his hands into them anyway, crunching his fingers into fists to loosen them up. Before trying to plant the piece of wood again, he dug a hole. It was hard to keep it narrow, hard not to dislodge too much of the surrounding soil. When he thought the hole was deep enough, he put the wood in. It stayed upright. He packed the loose dirt and sod around the base and stood back. Not bad. If he could get them all standing and stabilize them with some cross pieces, it might just hold. He separated out his longest pieces, and arranged them evenly in a circle, ramming them into the ground as hard as he could and packing them tightly.

It was almost dark, but he still had lots of work to do. He glanced at the light coming from inside the house and saw Jacqueline standing at the window, her opera glasses trained on him. He waved a flowery glove. She walked away into the shadows.

Between the pieces lodged in the ground, Theo planted shorter ones, digging a hole to match each shape—flat ends, wedges, edges rounded by the sea. The plywood bits, he decided not to use, and tossed them aside. He left a gap for an entrance.

When the circle was done, he took off the gloves and lit a cigarette. His wrists were sore. He was tired. He looked at the leftover wood. He wasn't sure it was going to be enough for the crosspieces. He looked at the bits of rope he'd brought from the garage, imagining a kind of fastening he might do with them, like he'd seen in pictures. He needed to think about how he would do this. He had a vision in mind of something organic, rustic, a long way from *Gone With the Wind*. And he needed to think about a roof. He needed to sit down.

He went to the terrace and lifted up one end of a deck chair, rolled it along, bumped it down the stairs and over the lawn to the half-finished gazebo. He pulled it through the opening and into the centre of the pillars. He lay on his back to think about the crosspieces and the roof. He looked at the sky and the few stars in view and wondered if a roof was necessary. *It's like Stonehenge*, he thought, *but with wood*. He crossed his ankles and closed his eyes.

* * *

Joy was tapping his feet with a broom. He propped himself up on his elbows and looked at the makeshift cage that surrounded him.

"You stink," Joy said, holding the broom upright and smiling down at him. "You're lucky she's not here right now. You have time to take a shower before she gets back. And clean up this mess."

The ground was littered with tools and the gardening gloves and empty beer bottles. Outside the cage was the stack of graffitied plywood and extra bits. It wasn't finished. Theo remembered now. He had fallen asleep thinking about a roof. *It doesn't look anything like Stonehenge*, he thought, surveying his work. But the pillars were still standing—that was good.

He looked at Joy, shielding his eyes from the sun. "How about a cup of coffee?" he said, grinning.

"Make your own coffee," she said, tapping him on the feet with her broom again. "I've got the whole house to do. And I need that chair."

THIRTY-FOUR

THEO CHECKED THE address. He had the right place. He locked the bike to a pole and took his helmet with him. It was an old brick building, six storeys high. He wasn't sure about this, wasn't sure he wanted to go through with it, but he was running out of ideas. There was an intercom at the entrance, but none of the buttons were labelled. Theo tried the door. It was unlocked. He stepped inside.

The smell was horrible, stale, sour, cigarettes, sweat, old carpet and lives that had been shut in too long. He took off his sunglasses and looked again at the message that Curtis had sent — fifth floor, door on the right. There was an elevator, but Theo decided to take the stairs. At each level, it got hotter, and by the time he reached the fifth floor, he was dripping. He stood on the landing and wiped his face with the bottom half of his T-shirt. He looked at the door on the right. No number. Paint peeling. He knocked. Waited. Knocked again.

"I wouldn't go in there if I were you," a voice said. Theo turned his head and saw a tall, slim, bald man leaning in the doorway of the apartment next door, his arms crossed casually. "Roaches. When they fumigated in the spring, Mr. Lee was too sick to leave his apartment, so they skipped his place. A week later, he passed on, and all the roaches moved in."

Theo stepped back from Mr. Lee's door.

"You know, after I met your friends the other night," the bald man said, "I came straight home and scoured the place for a photo of you. I was so certain I had one. But alas!"

So this is Sid, he thought. And that door must be the other *door on the right*.

"Come on in," Sid said. "No buggies here."

Theo followed him into the apartment. Sid closed the door behind them and locked it with three chains. It was bright inside. The windows shone. There was an air conditioner built into one of the windows, and the room was cool. It smelled a little of old wood, but not like the hallways. A neon sign hung from the ceiling in one corner — a pink martini, not lit up.

There was a lot to take in. Shelves of books, boxes, magazines, photographs, postcards, a glass vase filled with matchbooks, another with white roses, stacks of tape cassettes, video cassettes, CDs, everything neat and orderly but crammed into every inch, and not a speck of dust. There were footstools, several of them, flanking the shelves, upholstered in various shades of leather. And tucked in behind one of the bookshelves, up against the window, was a little desk with a laptop, open.

Sid brought two glasses of iced tea from the kitchen. Theo took a sip. It was strong and bitter, but wonderfully cold.

It was hard to tell how old Sid was. His face was lined, his yesterday beard was grey, but he moved like a younger man. He was wearing jeans and a short-sleeved shirt with roses embroidered on the chest. A rockabilly shirt. He had clear, blue eyes, serious eyes.

"So I couldn't find a picture of you, but I did find some of your mother." Sid picked up a folder and sat on one of the footstools.

"You mean Charlotte?" Theo asked.

Sid looked at Theo inquisitively, then his face lit up. "Right!" he said. "Of course! I'm so sorry. I never did have that straight."

He opened the folder. Theo sat down on a stool beside him, and Sid passed him a picture. It was Charlotte, on stage, in a long red dress. And another, different dress.

"She always had her own style," Sid said. "Never followed the trends."

Theo flipped through the pictures. They were all taken in the same place, at the foot of a small stage. In most of them, Charlotte was alone. In a few she had her arms around a couple of drag queens, fake eyelashes, puckered lips. Theo paused at one picture of Charlotte sitting in a dressing room. It looked as though whoever was taking the photograph had called her name and she'd turned to look. Her eyes were bright. She was smiling, almost laughing. She had a tube of lipstick in her hand. And there was a mirror behind her, and in the mirror, you could see her back, and part of the person taking the photograph, and further in the distance someone hanging something up or taking something down from a wall of shiny gowns. In the picture, Charlotte looked the way Theo had always remembered.

"Would you mind if I kept this one?" he asked.

"Be my guest. And there's another one, let me see if I can find it." He shuffled through the folder. "This one! I want you to give this to Charlotte for me." He handed it to Theo. "Wasn't I gorgeous?"

"That's you?" Theo stared at the picture. "But you ..."

"Don't look like a man, I know," Sid said. "And so young!"

In the picture Charlotte had her hand on Sid's shoulder. She was standing on her tiptoes, and Sid was leaning in for a kiss on the cheek. Both of them were winking at the camera. Theo looked at Sid sitting beside him now, then back at the picture.

"Your friend," Sid said. "He mentioned something about a dilemma."

"Yeah. Yeah. That's right. I ... I hope you don't mind. He thought it might help. I don't know, I just ..." Theo took a deep breath and sat up straight. "It's Charlotte. She's not speaking. Or singing. For weeks."

Sid studied him.

"She's become silent," Theo explained. "And Jacqueline, the French lady, the one with the house, you know, where we're living, she's insisting that I make Charlotte sing, which is ridiculous because you can't just make a person do something, can you?"

"No," Sid said. "No, you can't." He was frowning, shaking his head slightly. "Jacqueline?" he asked, looking up. "Jacqueline Day?"

"Yeah. I don't think she's doing Charlotte any good."

"Unbelievable," Sid said. He put his glass on a shelf and the folder on the floor. He pressed the heels of his hands onto his knees and shook his head some more. "First of all. She's not French."

"What?"

"She's not French. Jacqueline. The French lady. She's a fake."

"What do you mean?"

"She's a Brit who lived in France when she was younger and likes to pass herself off as a Parisian and has done a very good job at it. Everybody eats it up. Everybody wants to be a little closer to Paris."

"What?" Theo couldn't believe it. It didn't make sense. Why would someone do that? And what about Olivier? He must have known. And the accent. And the way she talked. And the stories. Why would she do that? "Wow. That's crazy. And people don't know?"

"Oh sure, lots of people know. But they just go along with it. Let her believe that *they* believe. All part of the charade. Frankly, I can't believe she's still around. But hey, why not? I'm still around."

Theo was holding the little stack of photos. He looked again at the one on top — Sid in drag. The illusion was remarkable.

"I never had the privilege of knowing Jacqueline Day," Sid said. "But I had a friend who did. He dropped me as soon as he figured out how to roll with the money. Came back to visit once, showed me his custom-made shirt. It was the last time I saw him." Sid stood up, hunched a little now. He looked older. He was facing the books on the shelves and trailed his fingers along the spines to make them flush.

"I told myself that Charlotte was better off, but in my heart of hearts, I knew it wasn't true. Business was bad, and I couldn't use her anymore. But it wasn't just about the money. Your father was gone. You were gone. She was devastated. Broken. And vulnerable. Needy. Too needy for me. All I could think about was how she was bringing me down. Back then everything had to be up, up, up." He turned and looked at Theo. "She was my friend, and I didn't care enough to see it. Doesn't make me any better than the custom-made shirt, does it?"

Theo swirled the ice cubes in the bottom of his glass then took a long, last sip. His heart was full, heavy. He didn't know what he was going to do about Charlotte, but he felt right in himself, reassured somehow. He stood up and stretched his arms behind his head. He needed to move.

As he watched Sid put the two photographs in a yellow envelope, he thought about how he had never asked his father for a picture of his real mother, and how his father had never bothered to give him one. Theo knew they existed. He'd seen them once in a drawer. But he'd convinced himself that he didn't care.

The stench and heat of the hallway hit him, and he tried not to breathe more than he had to. Sid handed him the envelope and told him to come back any time. They shook hands. Sid watched Theo leave, and Theo wondered if he was going to wave like people do in doorways or on porches or at the end of driveways, but he didn't wave. Theo bounded down the first flight of stairs.

"And don't forget," Sid called out. "That friend of yours, Curtis …"

"I know, I know," Theo called back, already at the third floor, "he's the best friend I could ever have!"

THIRTY-FIVE

THEO WAS TALKING too fast, talking about Jacqueline, it was all a lie, manipulation. "And I'm not going to waste my time," he said. "Just let her keep on pretending." And he was talking about leaving, getting out. And Charlotte was supposed to go with him. Maybe she could stay with Curtis, he said, until she found a place of her own. He'd talk to Curtis. He was sure it would be okay. Just for a little while. "Everything will be fine," he kept saying. "We'll figure it out."

Charlotte was trying to keep up. The photograph she held in her lap, the one of her and Sid, it was another world, another time, left behind, and now Theo was talking about things in between, and things to come. The club had turned into a karaoke bar, Theo said. She knew that. Then it was torn down, and condos were built.

"We can go see him," Theo said. Charlotte tried to make sense of it, tried to pull the threads together—Sid in the picture, svelte, tanned, lots of leg, and Sid the way Theo described him now, serious, sober, masculine, and the club, what it used to be, red bricks, all knocked down. She couldn't get past the heap of bricks in her mind, an empty lot in the city block, dust and weeds and rubble.

"It's too hot," Theo said. "You have to open this window." He put his hand on the latch. Charlotte stood up. He looked at her and let go. He paced. He looked in corners that were empty. Charlotte watched, wishing she could calm him, reassure him.

"Today she asked me if you were going to be ready. I didn't know what to say. She's going to kick me out. I know it. And frankly I don't care. I really don't care. I'd just rather get myself out of here before she has a chance to get rid of me." He stopped pacing. "But I can't leave without you. And I don't know what she'll do. I don't know what she expects."

I don't want you to stay just for me. Charlotte's words pushed but couldn't get out.

Theo looked at her feet, her satin slippers. "Shoes!" he shouted. "Where are your shoes?" He went to the closet and yanked the doors open. "Here!" He pulled a pair from the shelf. "You need shoes!"

Charlotte didn't move. She looked at the shoes he held out. They weren't shoes at all, but another pair of slippers, with a little bow and kitten heels. She watched Theo's face. He seemed to understand. His brows furrowed. His eyes flared. He chucked them on the floor and grabbed another pair. More slippers. Chucked them too. Stilettos. With rhinestones. Sequins. Straps. Suede. Silk. Still more slippers. Theo threw each pair behind him, no longer stopping to look at what they were.

A shoe hit Charlotte on the shin. She stepped back, started to cry. Theo grabbed the last pair in the closet and held them out in his hands, a mad offering. They were gorgeous. Covered in crystals. Charlotte remembered Jacqueline giving them to her. She had worn them only once. They were so rigid she could barely walk in them. Theo was holding them out to her now, begging her to take them. A bead of sweat dropped from his forehead onto one of the shoes and glistened among the crystals.

"You can't live like this," he said, his voice low, his words slow and deliberate. "It's too damned hot!" He dropped the shoes, and Charlotte dropped the picture she had been clutching and caught the shoes. Theo rushed to the wasp window and thrust it open. Particles rained down, and Charlotte held up the shoes to protect her face.

But there was no swarm. No rush. No angry buzz. Just a cloud of smoky grey flakes, the abandoned wasp nest bust into a thousand pieces.

Charlotte had stopped crying. A faint breeze filtered through the room. Theo smiled, Charlotte smiled back, and they started to laugh.

"You couldn't even scream *no*!" Theo said. "Could you?"

Charlotte shook her head, laughing even more in her funny, silent way. The floor was scattered with shoes and slippers, shiny and useless, all of them.

After a while they stopped laughing and caught their breath. Theo had slid down onto the floor and sat with his knees bent, his back against the wall, under the open window. Charlotte put the crystal shoes back in the closet.

"Last night I tried to build the gazebo," Theo said. "But it's just a bunch of posts stuck in the ground." Charlotte sat down on the edge of her bed. "I'm not very good at finishing things. People always say that about me. And I always want to prove them wrong. Then I don't."

He reached forward and picked up the photograph of Charlotte and Sid. "I just didn't want to see it anymore," he said. "All that wood. Lying around."

Theo stood up and handed the picture to Charlotte. He went back to the wasp window, stuck his head out and looked up to where the nest had been built on the edge of the window frame. The outline of the nest was still there, adhered to the wood, in a pattern like the veins of a leaf. He drew his head back in, walked over to the fan, adjusted it, waited a bit, feeling for a current of air, adjusted it again.

"Everything will be fine," he said. "We'll figure it out."

THIRTY-SIX

JACQUELINE INTRODUCED THEM, but of course they'd already met. Charlotte remembered Jeremiah from the performance that had caused all the trouble. She had sat hidden on the landing afterwards listening to him play well into the night. At the moment, however, Jacqueline was acting as though there hadn't been any trouble, as though nothing was wrong, as though nothing was out of the ordinary, and Charlotte had the sensation of time being erased, the history, the facts, erased and replaced by courtesies, vacant smiles.

As she watched Jacqueline, she tried to *see* her, see her more clearly. She hadn't been surprised when Theo had told her that Jacqueline wasn't French. Confused, yes. Curious. And hurt. But not surprised. Charlotte watched Jacqueline, but Jacqueline didn't make eye contact.

Jeremiah declined the tea that was offered. He clutched his books under one arm. His glasses kept slipping down his nose, and he kept pushing them back up. He looked highly uncomfortable, but alert.

Jacqueline left the room abruptly. Jeremiah sat on the piano bench and opened a book, and Charlotte understood. It was an ambush.

"I'm primarily classical," Jeremiah said, leafing through

the music. "But I've taken a look at some of this and it shouldn't be a problem. Is there anything you have in mind?"

Charlotte didn't move.

"Why don't I just play a few things, and you can tell me what you like?" He pushed his glasses up and started to play.

Charlotte wasn't listening. Her head buzzed hot. Swelled. Jacqueline had tricked her. Asked her to come downstairs under false pretences, then thrown her in front of this poor young man who probably had no clue what was going on.

What does she want from me? What does she want? Charlotte put her hand to her forehead. It was real, the heat. There was burning. And clamouring from inside. *I'm a mouth*, she thought. *That's all that I am to her. Just a mouth. To open and close when she wants. A mouth. And a voice. I could be anybody.*

She ran her hand over her forehead, smoothing back strands of hair. She started to breathe more slowly now. She started to feel calmer. She looked at Jeremiah and wondered if she was expected to sing out of pity. *What an awful trick, using him like this*, she thought.

He played with his shoulders raised and neck stiff, peering at the pages, so different from Olivier. And Charlotte questioned whether Jacqueline cared even about Olivier, or whether he was expendable too. Through the terrace doors, she could see the shape of Theo's gazebo, the ring of posts, and thought about what he'd said earlier that day—wanting to start over. She wondered where he was. The beach probably. She was glad he was out. He needed to be out. She knew how hard it was for him to stay.

After a few songs, Jeremiah stopped and swung his legs

around. He took off his glasses and cleaned them hastily on his shirt.

"Jacqueline said this might happen," he said quietly. *So he does know*, Charlotte thought. *Good*. "I think ... Well, I'm not sure. I'm not sure what she's going to want me to do, but maybe I can leave these books here, and you can have a look if you like, and we'll see tomorrow?"

His voice was shaking. He stood up and put his glasses back on, pressing them against the bridge of his nose with his index finger. He glanced down the hall. Charlotte felt sorry for him. He was ready to leave but couldn't yet. She walked over to where he stood, gently touched his elbow and led him towards Jacqueline's office. She left him there, in the hallway, to knock.

* * *

Charlotte closed the door to her room, held it shut. Could she really leave?

Her room had been tidied. How odd. She could tell by the bed. The quilt had been straightened, the pillows arranged. Was Joy in the house? She was usually gone by then. There was a dress hanging over the mirror, one that Charlotte had never seen. She approached it, warily, touched the bodice, ran her fingers over the stitching. It was exquisite. On the floor were the crystal shoes. The ones she'd put back in the closet. The ones that Theo had dropped and she had caught. They were on the floor now, at the foot of the mirror. The dress was on a hanger, and the hanger stuck out of her reflection, stuck right out of her neck and hooked over the top of the mirror.

I'm the trouble, she thought. *I'm still in the way. I tried to get out of the way, but I'm still here.*

There was a breeze. Theo had created a good cross-draft by re-angling the fan.

* * *

"I refuse," Theo insisted into his phone. "I will not be swayed. Wild horses ..."

Curtis was trying to convince him to come over, just for the night, sleep it off, but Theo was adamant that he wouldn't leave Charlotte alone.

"Wild horses ..."

"You're no good to her like this," Curtis said.

"I'm fine!" Theo stood up from the log where he'd been sitting but pitched forward. His knees hit the sand, sunk in. "I'm praying," he said into the phone.

"What?"

"I'm praying," he said again, laughing. His knees were anchored in the sand, and he was leaning back, his right hand holding the phone to his ear, his left hand stretching up to the dark. Stoned and grinning, he *was* praying, giving thanks. "I'm so lucky. I have all this." He motioned with his free hand to the sky and the sea. The party was still going on down the beach, quieter now. They didn't want the cops to come. The tide was in, and the waves churned. The air too.

"Can you get yourself home?" Curtis asked.

"Eventually."

THIRTY-SEVEN

CHARLOTTE OPENED THE closet in the front hall. There was a row of Jacqueline's shoes, and a pair of Olivier's, but nothing that belonged to her. She dipped her toe into one of Jacqueline's loafers but couldn't bring herself to put it on. She crouched down and reached past a couple of long coats and a cardboard box full of something heavy. In the back, her hand landed on what she was hoping to find—her garden clogs. She pulled them out and gently closed the closet door, not wanting to wake anyone.

Blades of grass, wet from the sprinklers, slipped into the back of her clogs and around the curves of her feet as she walked across the lawn. *So this is it*, she thought, stopping at the gazebo. Theo was right—it wasn't much of a gazebo. It was barely a fort. But at least yesterday when she'd looked at it from inside the house, it was standing upright. This morning most of the posts were askew, some fallen right over.

Charlotte entered the circle through an opening, careful not to bump anything, and sat down on a small stump in the middle. She looked at the cigarette butts at her feet and the half-collapsed walls, the spaces between the posts and the dark sky above, not just dark with night, but dark with cloud. She laughed at the fact that, on the day she'd finally decided to come outside, the sun had gone into hiding.

The air prickled. She was being watched. A coyote stood outside the gazebo, staring at her.

"Isn't it your bedtime?" Charlotte asked the coyote.

They were both surprised by the sound of her voice. It was real sound. Out-loud sound. Charlotte touched her lips in amazement. The coyote's ears twitched. Charlotte lowered her hand, and the coyote dropped its guard a little, putting its nose to the ground to sniff. Charlotte had never been this close to a coyote. It was best to leave them alone or shoo them away, but this one, she wanted it to stay and talk.

"You can't talk," she said. The coyote cocked its head. Charlotte smiled a great big smile. "But I can."

The coyote lifted a front paw then strode off, across the grass, looking back at Charlotte once before ducking through a gap below the fence and into the shadow of the forest.

Charlotte wanted to tell the coyote things. Things about Theo. That she knew Theo was staying just for her. And that she didn't want him to. Nobody would be happy that way. Not Theo. Not her. She wanted to tell the coyote that she didn't want to stay either. And that if anything was going to change, she had to make it happen.

She sat on the stump, thinking about all the things she would say to the coyote, occasionally whispering words out loud to make sure they were still there. She continued like this until the last of the night had disappeared, until there was nothing left but grey day. Even without the sun, the morning heat was thick. Trapped for so many weeks, it pushed for space.

She looked at the house. There were logistical problems. Questions of where and how. Where would she go? How would she live? She had nothing. No money. No family. She couldn't rely on Theo. It wasn't fair. Or realistic. She would just have to figure it out. She looked at the house again. The thought of going back inside was not appealing, but she needed a few things. She'd have to be quick.

What did she need? Clothes, hairbrush, toothbrush, towel, the photograph from Sid, the piece of paper with Theo's phone number, and the postcard that had just arrived from Olivier, palm trees on the Côte d'Azur. And a coat. The packings of a runaway. In her mind she located each item in the house and determined the order in which they should be retrieved. She needed a bag. She thought about a bag, where she would find one. Had she seen a bag in the front hall closet? Jacqueline's plaid shopping bag?

What would Jacqueline say?

Charlotte leaned forward and took hold of a fallen post. She stood up and slotted it back in its hole. It teetered. She grabbed it again and jammed it in as hard as she could. It stuck. She did the same with each piece of wood that had toppled over, driving them into the ground with all her strength. Some of them continued to lean a little, and some were just naturally bent, warped relics of the sea.

The clouds were thick now. There was a mounting pressure in the air. Charlotte heard a rumble of thunder far in the distance.

"Jacqueline doesn't get to say," she said. "Not anymore."

Up on the terrace, on the shelf of a side table, Charlotte found exactly what she was looking for—a matchbook. She went back to the circle and lit a match. The flame surged, but when she put it to a post, it went out. She lit a second match. That one burned longer but went out too. Something was needed to get the fire going. She rummaged near the bushes at the side of the house, gathering an armload of dried weeds and twigs. She sprinkled these around the base of the posts in a ring. She lit a third match. There was a spark in the weeds, then a flame, then the flame spread from weed to weed and to the twigs, which crackled when they caught fire. Before long, one of the posts was burning.

Charlotte hurried into the house. Clogs in hand, she took the stairs two at time on the balls of her feet. First she stopped at the bathroom and grabbed the things she needed from there. She'd forgotten about getting a bag first. She looked under the sink and found a white plastic garbage bag. She dumped everything into that. Then she nipped across the hall to her bedroom and gathered the remaining items on her mental list, emptying a straw basket of scarves to contain it all. Thunder rocked the sky. She froze, waited. Two long seconds went by, then the room lit up, and she caught sight of herself in the mirror. Her face was flushed. And the gorgeous new gown hung exactly where it had, as though petrified in time, the crystal shoes set neatly below.

That's when it sunk in, what she had done.

She moved silently, swiftly, back down the stairs, balanced with basket and clogs. *Coyote, coyote, coyote, coyote*, she intoned in her head. The posts were ablaze. Sparks floated upwards. What had she done? What if it spread? What if the forest caught fire? Or the house?

"What have I done?"

The sky growled in response. The flames were alive and grasping, clawing. Thunder cracked through the thick air and rattled the terrace boards under Charlotte's feet. The grey clouds lit up, the sky opened, and it poured.

Finally, it poured.

Charlotte let the rain beat down on her head, squeezing the straw basket to her chest. She could go now.

THIRTY-EIGHT

FOR A WHILE he was still in the dream, and the noise was a guitar smashing on a window from the inside of a room, a sound booth—he was trying to get out—but his head, the pain, it was real—his temples throbbed. Crash! Theo opened his eyes. Outside—creaks, rushes of air. He couldn't place them. Then another crash. The sound of thunder.

His eyes focused on the bed sheets, covered with dirt. His arms were smeared black, his chest too, marked with lines and crude images smudged beyond recognition. And then it came back to him—the beach and the bits of wood made into charcoal, tools for drawing. Had they built a fire? On the beach? No, that was crazy. They wouldn't have. The city was all dried up. No, he remembered now. One of the girls had burnt the end of a cork with her lighter and pressed it onto her cheek, making a big black dot. That's how it had started.

Another roar of thunder shook the room. There was a flash of lightning. Then a pounding noise, great waves of pounding. *Rain*, he thought. That was the sound of rain. He curled up on his side, facing the window. The half-open curtains fluttered in the stream of cool air.

"Theo!" It was Jacqueline screaming from the hallway. Banging on his door. "Get up! Get up! Outside!" He dragged himself out of bed and over to the window, his head searing. What now? He drew back the curtains.

Holy fuck. Flames shot through the rain. It was unbelievable. Like a ring of torches. *War torches*, he thought. A siege. Or a sacrifice, a ritual burning. He'd never seen anything like it. He scrambled into a pair of shorts and ran downstairs.

Jacqueline stood on the terrace under the eaves, wrapped in a big woven shawl. Theo ran right past her into the rain and was soaked in seconds. The fire was struggling to survive. Theo wanted it to survive, but already flames were starting to fizzle out, and a couple of the larger pieces of driftwood remained unlit, heavy with salt water. *Burn*, he thought. *Burn*. He wanted the fire to blaze. He wanted it to gobble up the gazebo, consume it, leave nothing but ashes. And then, the rain would stop. And the sun would come out. He pictured Joy, in the aftermath, sucking up ashes from the plush lawn with her fancy vacuum while the rest of them sipped cocktails on the terrace. No more gazebo. Clean slate.

But that wasn't going to happen, was it?

Several posts burned on in spite of the rain, and Theo could barely tell what was going which way, the elements knitting together in opposition, banding into a slick, fiery, roar. Then the rain itself seemed to ignite and hurl itself at the earth. The flames faltered under the assault. Theo ran for cover under the eaves. One by one, the posts went black. There were threads of smoke. And the smell of char. And the smell of the rain that hadn't come in weeks.

"Bravo!" Jacqueline yelled over the downpour. "Bravo!" She was clapping in mock tribute. Theo looked away, blood rising to his face. Out of the corner of his eye, he could see her adjusting her shawl, flinging one end over her shoulder with a flourish as she turned to go back inside. "You're lucky!" she yelled. "Extremely lucky!"

Theo shuddered in the chill of the rain. He looked at his bare chest, dripping grey with the ruined markings and realized what it must look like. The evidence was right there on his skin. *No wonder*, he thought. *She thinks I did it. She thinks I started the fire*. He squeezed his arms tight over his chest. It couldn't have been. It didn't add up. The markings were from the beach. He knew that. He remembered it clearly. Or at least he thought he did. He came home. Parked the bike. Walked around the side of the house and went right into the gazebo. He remembered that. He remembered staying there awhile, watching the sky. There were no stars. Maybe it was a cigarette. Maybe he didn't put out his cigarette. The thought of it made him sick to his stomach. He stared at the black remnants of the gazebo. *Lucky*.

He tracked water across the living room floor, up the stairs and into the bathroom. He started at the sight of himself in the mirror. His face ran with the same black mess that covered his body. It was a horrible face. Someone had tried to draw a smile on him, a big clown smile, and big eyebrows.

"Clown," he said to his reflection. The reflection didn't laugh. And then it did. And the effect of the tragic face laughing out loud made him laugh even harder, and he imagined riding over to Curtis' house with his clown face, riding through the city streets, people pointing and laughing as he went by. Maybe he'd wave. Ride with no hands. *Look at me, look at me, no hands!* He laughed more and

186 · SUZANNE CHIASSON

more at the thought of it and collapsed over the counter with his head in hands until finally he wasn't laughing anymore but crying.

It was always the same thing. He always had such good intentions.

He took a cloth and some soap and washed off the charcoal. He dried himself all over with a towel, but his shorts were saturated. *What a clown*, he said to himself. *What a fucking clown.*

* * *

Theo knocked gently on Charlotte's door. There was no answer. He opened it, expecting to see her outline under the covers of the bed. But the bed was empty.

"Charlotte?"

He went in. She wasn't there. A fresh coolness swept the room. Grey flakes from the shattered wasp nest shivered on the window ledge. Theo noticed the gown hung on the mirror and the crystal shoes below and the white slippers sitting neatly beside the bed. The room felt different without Charlotte there.

He searched the house but couldn't find her. The backyard was deserted. The rain fell more easily now, streaming down on the black posts. Rivulets of water ran in every direction, filling in cracks and pooling over dips in the land. Already there were puddles. Theo went back inside and upstairs. The taps were running in the master bathroom. He opened Jacqueline's bedroom door a crack to have a look. "Charlotte," he whispered, but no Charlotte. He was starting to get worried.

This time he went out the front door. He stood on the porch, keeping out of the rain. He breathed in the new air, tinged with the smell of soil and iron. Charlotte was gone. He knew it. He could feel it. She was gone.

He wondered where she would go, in this weather. He wondered if she had a coat. And he wondered what she was wearing on her feet.

THIRTY-NINE

"**I** HAVE NO idea where she is," Theo said, cramming clothes into his backpack. Jacqueline had appeared in the doorway out of nowhere.

"Really?" she asked. "You have no idea?"

"Nope."

"She'll be back. Foolish. You'd be foolish to leave too."

Theo stopped packing for a second. It was incredible. After everything—the fire, the gazebo, the silence he couldn't fix—Jacqueline wanted him to stay?

"A lot of missed opportunities," she said.

"Really? Like the last opportunity you gave me? You know your buddy the director—he made a pass at me."

"That's just his way."

"Well, it's not my way."

"*Non*?"

Theo turned back to his clothes, practically punching them into the bag. He wasn't going to be that person. He refused to be that person, just using people and taking off. That's what Jacqueline did. That's what his dad did. And that's exactly what he'd started to do with Curtis.

"*Non*!" he shot back. It sounded so stupid when he said it and he wished he hadn't. He thought of calling Jacqueline on her bullshit French, but there was something satisfying about holding back this little piece of information, a secret reminder to himself of what she was.

He cinched his pack shut and slung it over his shoulder. It was heavy, even without the shiny shoes left behind in the closet—he couldn't stand the sight of them. At first he'd left out the tuxedo as well, figuring he wasn't going to take any more charity, but then he thought *fuck it* and grabbed it off the hanger.

Theo took a step toward the doorway, but Jacqueline didn't move. He didn't want to touch her, didn't want any tiny part of his body touching any tiny part of hers.

"You will see," she said. "After a time you will see what you have lost."

"No, I think it's the other way around." He was inches from her face. "Because you know what? She loved you."

Jacqueline went white, dropped her gaze, steadied herself against the door frame. Theo held his pack out in front of him so it didn't touch her as he passed.

* * *

He went around the side of the garage to get the bike, hoping the overhang had kept it dry. But it was gone. The bike. He stared at the spot where he'd put it. He always put it in the same place. He walked around the garage, no bike. He opened the door to the garage and looked in, not there. Damn.

Then a thought occurred to him. Of course. The perfect getaway.

As the idea settled in his mind, he liked it more and more—Charlotte sailing down the driveway, past closed gates and long green lawns, around the curve at the end of the street and down, down toward the ocean.

Theo followed on foot, in the steady rain.

Acknowledgements

My SINCERE GRATITUDE to Guernica and its team, including editor Lindsay Brown for her faith in this book.

Thank you to Rachelle Kanefsky and Carol Watterson from Behind the Book for their kind and expert guidance.

Many thanks to friends, old and new, who have asked questions, read manuscripts, attended readings, and encouraged me along the way.

Charlotte Teeple Salas (not the Charlotte of this story) and Drue Neel Glauber, my sisters-in-writing, thank you for the journey. It's not over.

Gratitude to my parents and to all of my family for their love and support. Thanks to Jack and Esmé for keeping me laughing. And to Craig, for always believing in me.

About the Author

Suzanne Chiasson is a Vancouver novelist and poet. *Tacet* is her first novel.